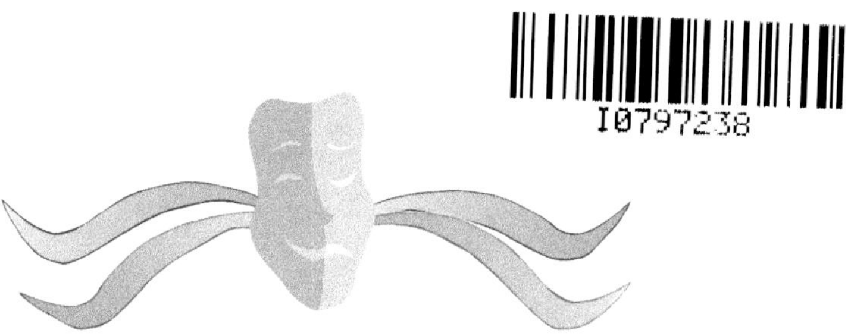

"Twice in one <u>day</u>, Thony?"

Even Princess Joanna's ever-patient tone sounded exasperated.

"What are you trying to do? Get Papa to keep you from ever seeing the light of day again? At this rate even Master Eswith will run out of protocol lessons."

"Um, no...?" She'd phrased it as a question, but Thony had the feeling it was rhetorical.

"And now you're involving the *servants* in your pranks again?" And *that* was disappointment, and if there was anyone whom Thony actually *cared* about not disappointing, it was his eldest sister.

"It wasn't a prank! The frog just sort of... escaped. And I knocked over her bucket. And then she helped catch it." Which was all true, if slightly out of order. And definitely gave the impression that the frog had been *his* to start, rather than that *he* had been the victim of the *girl's* prank.

There didn't seem to be any good way out of this one. Thony looked at his feet. The servant girl had the frog, so he couldn't even pretend he was looking at it.

Everyone in the castle tended to assume that, if there was something crazy going on, he was probably the cause of it.

To be fair, they were usually right.

And it was his honor and his privilege to liven things up a little.

...even if it <u>did</u> extend those interminable lessons with Master Eswith.

THONY AND THE MUCH-ANTICIPATED ADVENTURE

Book One of the Prankster Prince

KERRIDWEN MANGALA MCNAMARA

This book is a work of fiction. Names, characters, places, and incidents are the product of the author's imagination or are used fictitiously. Any resemblance to actual events, places or people, living or dead, is coincidental.

Also available in eBook and hardcover editions.
McNamara, Kerridwen Mangala
Thony and the Much-Anticipated Adventure / by Kerridwen Mangala McNamara Indiana: Rising Dragon Books, 2023
p. 176
(McNamara, Kerridwen Mangala. The Prankster Prince; bk. 1)
Summary: Fifteen-year-old Crown Prince, and inveterate prankster, Thony decides to go on a quest to find a princess to marry in order to save his country.
ISBN 978-1-960160-09-6 (pbk)
1. Princes and princesses - Fiction. 2. Adolescent Rebellion - Fiction
ISBN 978-1-960160-10-2 (hc) ISBN 978-1-960160-08-9(eBook)

Cover art and illustrations by the author
The Rising Dragon Logo was designed by Priyadevi McNamara

For further information, email RisingDragonBooks@gmail.com

ISBN: 978-1-960160-09-6
First Print Edition: June 2023
10 9 8 7 6 5 4 3 2 1

For my kids:
Meenakshi, Priya, Griffin, Rhodri, Miles, and Tara.
Without you guys, life wouldn't be half as much fun - nor would I be half the writer I am today.

And for Shawn Michael McNamara
(1950-2023)
Thank you for being a great father-in-law, grandfather, and for raising my husband to be the man he is. I miss your wisdom, strength, and sense of humor so much already.

CONTENTS

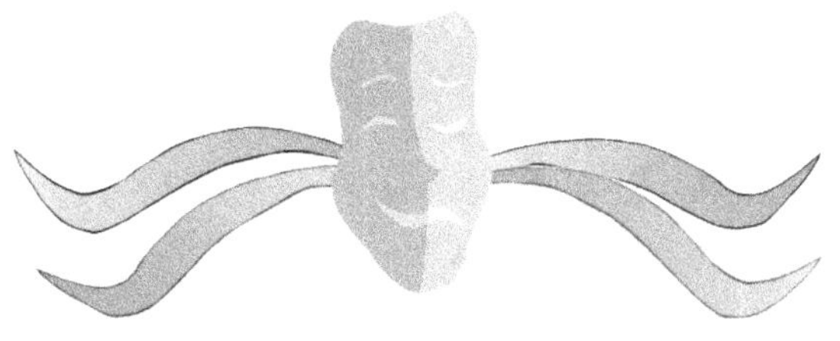

Chapter ONE

A Princely Punch

CROWN PRINCE ANTHONY DEVINTHAL THE AFFABLE (and the Affirmative) of the valley-kingdom of Aldyrwald – an inconsequential kingdom on a substandard continent on an unimportant world – slouched along a corridor of his father's castle, kicking a small rock that someone *(probably him)* had tracked into the castle earlier.

It wasn't *fair.*

His parents were ridiculously overprotective – all because Thony was Heir to the Throne. Queen Annabel had vapors when Thony went out of sight of the castle, even into the *very safe and well-maintained* woods beyond the village. King Bill started to *harumph* and look pale when Thony casually suggested a visit to the next valley-kingdom over, the one ruled by King Bill's best friend who also happened to be the father-in-law of Thony's older sister, Joanna – even *without* Thony hinting that a detour to check out the local giant along the way might be interesting.

Being a crown prince was *seriously boring*.

And anytime he tried to do something to *make* things a little less boring he ended up in trouble.

Today being a case in point.

It was his mother's fault really. She knew better than to come into his rooms.

For goodness' sake, the *servants* knew better than to come into his rooms.

Thony hadn't even been *in* there when Mama had opened the door, taken one look, screamed, and fainted.

Someone had been sensible enough to summon Joanna.

Someone *else* had tracked down Thony and seen him into the throneroom to face his father for a little chat about what King Bill called his 'misdemeanor'. *("You're the one who's meaner!" Thony had yelled in what was, perhaps, not the best display of behavior for a young man who was a few months away from fifteen. No matter that his parents seemed intent on treating him like he was five.)*

So now he was stuck with a fortnight of double-length protocol lessons with Master Eswith – the excruciatingly boring teacher who had reportedly convinced the eternally patient and polite Joanna to threaten to run away from home. *(That was the rumor anyways, passed on from Thony's middle sister, Priscilla. Joanna had been out from under Master Eswith's gentle care years before either of them had begun, though, so how Prissy knew this bit of intelligence was somewhat questionable.)*

An hour with Master Eswith was bad enough and what Thony had to suffer through on a regular basis. By two hours, the young prince was usually falling asleep and the 'gentle master' was beating him about the head and hands with a wooden ruler to *prove* that Thony had fallen asleep and Thony was plotting vengeance on Eswith and whichever parent had stuck him in double-length lessons. The one time King Bill had sentenced him to *three*-hour long lessons, Thony had plotted vengeance on the entire castle.

No one had ever considered doing that again, even though it had been almost five years and he'd grown a bit more of a sense of proportion. Apparently, the memory of caterpillars everywhere – in the bedsheets, in shoes, in the cabinets of clean dishes *(but not in the food. He wasn't an idiot after all)* – still lingered.

Thony kind of agreed that he'd deserved what he'd gotten for that one – helping clean up all the mess – but most of his pranks were much more amusing and innocuous. And he still got in trouble with his father over them. *(And honestly? How seriously could you take a man who let his subjects call him 'King Bill'? Thony had long ago decided that if anyone tried to call him 'King Thony' when he was crowned, he'd lop their heads off. Except his sisters. And their husbands; Roger and Jeremy were cool. And maybe his mother.)*

Princes were supposed to go on adventures and do interesting things. Instead, his *sisters* had gone off on The Quest a year earlier – and Left Him Behind. Instead, he'd been stuck *here* in *the most boring place in the Entire Universe.* And with no real hope that he would *ever* get to go *anywhere* or do *anything* interesting. *Ever.*

Of course, he didn't really blame his sisters *(or Prince Roger, the second-born prince from the neighboring kingdom)* for going on The Quest. They'd kind of had to, after the debacle that Prissy's sixteenth birthday party had become. But they'd left him behind.

They'd come back a few months later. Both of his sisters had gotten married while they were gone, though Mama and Papa had insisted that Joanna and Roger, at least, go through a second wedding ceremony *('for propriety's sake' – as if the very fact of Priscilla and Joanna secretly going off on The Quest hadn't taken everything so far beyond the pale of 'propriety' that there was no real way back. But the wedding had made Mama and Papa happier, not to mention King Richie and Queen Janet. Though Roger's older – and as yet unmarried – brother, Raymond, had kept giving both of the newlyweds odd looks as if he <u>wanted</u> to be happy for them, but couldn't quite stop wondering if they were planning to usurp the throne he was to inherit someday.)*

But Joanna had married *Roger*, whom they'd known forever. Mama and Papa were more or less refusing to acknowledge Priscilla's husband at all.

His sisters *(and Roger)* had also come back with the news that their magick-poor world was about to undergo a 'Ragnarök'. All the Gods they had been worshiping forever were about to *die* and be replaced by new ones. And the new ones just *happened* to be: Joanna and Roger and Priscilla – and the handful of friends they had brought back from The Quest.

Oh, and after all that, magick would be much more available to use. For everyone, not just the wisewomen and hermits and witches and sorcerers.

Mama and Papa's skepticism had been palpable. *(No one else than them and Thony had been told about the creation of new Gods at the time, although the word of the 'Ragnarök' had been duly passed along – no doubt with the tale growing less believable with every iteration.)* Princesses falling asleep for a hundred years and princes turning into swans and evil witches and ogres and such were par for the course in their opinion, but *Gods?*

And Joanna and Roger and Priscilla weren't even lucky-numbered children. Joanna was at least an eldest child, but she'd had the bad taste to then have a pair of younger siblings – nine years later, though apparently it hadn't been for lack of effort on King Bill and Queen Annabel's parts at attempting to properly produce three children *(of one gender)* or seven or twelve. *(Or even thirteen, though that number usually created more problems than it solved. King Bill was the oldest of seven brothers, and Queen Annabel was the youngest of seven sisters with three older brothers as well.)*

But Roger and Priscilla were both second-borns.

And then there was Prissy's tail.

Supposedly she'd been born the absolute epitome of perfect princesshood – golden-haired, bright blue eyes *(they were really more green, but for marketing purposes were blue)*, fair skin, the works. But somewhere in the handful of minutes between her birth and being Presented to the Populace, Priscilla had acquired a bushy, black tail that was nearly as long as she was.

When the tail had fallen out of her baby blankets during her Presentation to the Populace – and it was obviously attached to the baby – their father, King Bill, had fainted. *(Which wasn't a manly thing to do, but what can you do when the guy tells people to call him 'King Bill'?)*

*Un*fortunately, he'd been holding the baby.

Fortunately – despite all the adults frozen in horror around her – nine-year-old Princess Joanna was the only person who had the presence of mind to dash forwards and rescue her baby sister from their falling father. And then to stand up before all the people *(who had been seriously confused, I mean, nothing interesting ever happened here)* and declaim that it was a fine tail. That, in fact it was quite likely the finest tail a princess had ever had. And then she told everyone to call Prissy 'Princess

Priscilla the Bright-Eyed and Bushy-Tailed' *(which might be where all these ridiculous appellations attached to the royal children had gotten started, though at least Joanna had gotten 'the Wise and Wonderful'. Not that Thony begrudged his sisters theirs, but 'the Affable and the Affirmative'? Yeesh!)* and the poor, confused crowds had cheered enthusiastically.

That was all fine with the Local Populace and even their own minor nobility were willing to go along with things, but Word had gotten out *(Mama said Word always did)* and the royalty in all the neighboring kingdoms had decided the Devinthals had Bad Blood and decided to avoid them. Except for Roger's parents, of course, since King Richie and King Bill had been friends since they were boys.

But since the local nobility of a given valley tended to follow the lead of their king, it meant that all of King Bill's pages and squires were the scions of local families, and all of Queen Annabel's ladies-in-waiting were as well. This was potentially something of a problem, since the girls and boys were sent up to the castle to find a spouse as much as to learn some useful skills, but King Richie had traded them a couple *(which was how they'd gotten to know Roger so well in the first place, though it seemed likely he hadn't been granted permission from King Richie to ask for Joanna's hand – so perhaps even best-friendship only went so far in the matter of Bad Blood)* and if there were somewhat fewer of each group than the king and queen would like, because some of their own more remotely located nobility had sent *their* scions off to other kingdoms, it didn't bother *Thony* at all.

He was busy mulling over all this old history and the Utter Unfairness of having been Left Behind while his sisters had Adventures in the Fairy Wood and how his small attempts to liven up this deadly boring place were met with such an extreme underappreciation... So he wasn't really paying attention to where that rock was going and he nearly tripped over the girl scrubbing the floor.

Well.

Actually, his rock skittered into her bucket and knocked it over, even though he hadn't kicked it all *that* hard.

And *then* this midget-sized girl popped up practically under his chin and belted him a solid one in the gut.

And *then*, while he was stumbling away in surprise, he slipped in the soapy water and fell down, landing on top of the angry girl.

Who called him clumsy and overweight *(which he wasn't, thank you very much, either one. He'd been lanky until a couple years ago and now was sort of... stocky. Priscilla said he was just getting ready for a growth spurt, and she should know if anyone did, since she was now the Goddess of Animals – which apparently included humans, to Mama and Papa's even greater dismay)*.

She also called him a thoughtless oaf... and that one struck a bit closer to home, given that he knew that a prince should always be considerate of his People and he really *should* have been more aware of where that rock was going. But he hadn't, because he hadn't been paying attention. Which was sort of the whole problem in a nutshell.

And anyways the whole thing was just too embarrassing. Getting beaten up by a teeny little girl who looked like she was maybe ten – and him almost fifteen? That dinky thing had a right hook that out-sized her for sure! And if he should have to try to explain this to someone...

No. Nope. *Not* happening.

Thony had sloshed halfway down the corridor and almost around the corner when he realized there was something in his *pants*. Something that was *cold* and *wriggling* – and in his *under*pants, or it would have fallen out down his pantleg since Thony didn't hold with hose or tight pants.

It turned out to be a frog and it was alive and relatively unsquished when he got it out... which was a relief, though what he'd had to do to *get* it out in good order had been somewhat embarrassing.

That was when he heard the laughter.

He turned around and saw the scrubbing girl, hands on her hips, and laughing her head off at his antics.

Thony's first reaction was to scowl resentfully at her, but after a scant moment his expression changed to a sheepish grin. He'd stuffed enough frogs down other people's clothes *(though never their underpants – and how had she managed to do that without him noticing?)* that he had a fair idea of what he must have looked like. And it *was* pretty funny.

"He's getting away! Help me catch him!" The girl splashed sudsy water as she darted after the frog that was merrily hopping away from them.

Thony followed her without a question. Frogs – as pretty much everyone from Mama to Joanna to Priscilla had informed him on more than one occasion – *didn't* belong in the castle. The stone floors were too hard and dry for a creature that spent much of its life submerged in water, and the servants did too good a job at cleaning even the remotest dusty corners so there weren't enough insects for it to eat. *(Though Mama's concerns were rather different than his or his sisters'.)*

And chasing a frog through the castle together was generally silly enough to make anyone either fast friends or mortal enemies.

Honestly, Thony didn't care which. Either one would lighten the incredible boringness of life in Aldyrwald.

Fortunately, they caught up with the frog just inches before it would have leapt into his mother's solarium to wreak havoc on ladies-in-waiting and embroidery hoops alike.

Not so fortunately, Mama came over to see the commotion at the door, spotted the frog, and fainted. Again.

Joanna was sent for and Thony and the girl were made to wait for her while the ladies-in-waiting waved smelling salts under Queen Annabel's nose and placed cold cloths on her head and gossiped in quiet, giggly voices.

"Twice in one *day*, Thony?" Even Joanna's ever-patient tone sounded exasperated. "What are you trying to do? Get Papa to keep you from ever seeing the light of day again? At this rate even Master Eswith will run out of protocol lessons."

"Um, no...?" She'd phrased it as a question, but Thony had the feeling it was rhetorical.

"And now you're involving the *servants* in your pranks again?" And *that* was disappointment, and if there was anyone whom Thony actually *cared* about not disappointing, it was Joanna.

"It wasn't a prank! The frog just sort of... escaped. And I knocked over her bucket. And then she helped catch it." Which was all true, if slightly out of order. And definitely gave the impression that the frog had been *his* to start, rather than that *he* had been the victim of the *girl's* prank.

There didn't seem to be any good way out of this one. Thony looked at his feet. The girl had the frog, so he couldn't even pretend he was looking at it.

Priscilla bustled up right then – presumably summoned by Joanna in that God-Way they had now, or else called by the frog in her role as Goddess of Animals. She plucked the frog out of the girl's hands and headed back out, cooing at it, and only noticing Thony by way of a quick ruffling of his red curls. She had that look she got when someone interrupted what Thony had nicknamed 'Jeremy-time' – though apparently part of being a Goddess was the ability to appear perfectly turned out in a proper, princessly pink and frilly daygown when one might be seen by one's mother and her ladies.

So much for his best friend since forever.

Jeremy was cool, of course – and how cool was it to have a *centaur* for a brother-in-law? – but Priscilla never had time for Thony anymore.

"The bucket got tipped over? I'd imagine that's how the frog escaped – and why the pair of you are dripping suds," Joanna said thoughtfully after Priscilla had disappeared.

Her eyes looked like she had rather more of an idea of what had happened than that... like she could just look into Thony's own *soul* and pull the truth right out of him. And maybe she really *could*, now that she was the Goddess of the Earth and all. Though she'd been giving him *that* kind of look pretty much ever since he'd first discovered frogs when he was two or three years old, so it might just be a Joanna-Thing and not a Goddess-Thing.

"I should probably get that water taken care of and finish cleaning the floor before anyone slips in it and gets hurt," the girl suggested. Thony decided he needed to remember that little crease between the brows that did such an excellent job of suggesting Concern and Responsibility. Not that it would likely do *him* much good, given that everyone in the castle tended to assume that if there was something crazy going on he was probably the cause of it.

To be fair, they were usually right.

And it was his honor and his privilege to liven things up a little.

Even if it did extend those interminable lessons with Master Eswith.

Joanna looked at him with a fair amount of empathy. "I'll tell you what, Thony, you go help this girl clean up all that soapy water and we'll just call it even. I'll make things right with Mama."

That was... not entirely unexpected. Joanna's approach to discipline was all about 'natural consequences', which translated into 'fixing what you'd messed up'. And since cleaning up the messes he'd helped create was *far and away* more interesting than protocol lessons, Thony far preferred it when *she* got to sort him out.

However, he did kind of have to admit that King Bill's approach was probably a more effective deterrent. Not only did it leave the energetic young prince less time to think up new ways to create havoc, but adding to the overall boringness of Aldyrwald – especially in his own personal life – went against every principle he tried to live by.

Though if he managed to stay *awake* while listening to Master Eswith droning on about what fork to use at dinner for which esoteric side-dish that would probably never show up on Thony's plate, he often could daydream up some of his best ideas. Unfortunately, Master Eswith dealt with daydreaming about the same as he did actual sleeping, and bruises from that ruler could really hurt.

"Thanks, Joanna, you're the best!" He stretched up and gave her a kiss on the cheek, then trotted after the girl. She'd taken Joanna's comment as a permission to leave and had almost disappeared around a corner already. He had to move fast to catch up.

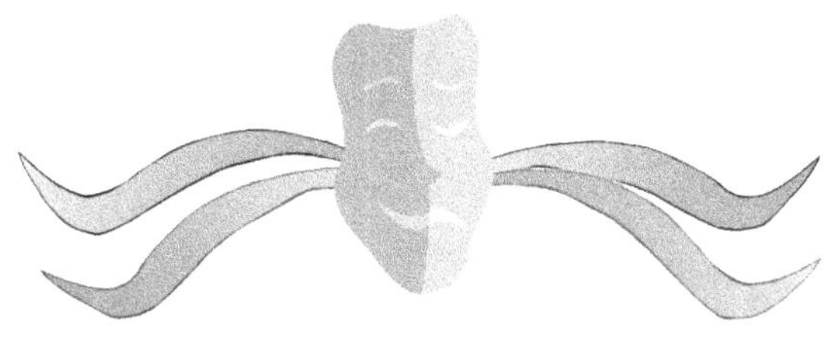

Chapter TWO

Oh... *Rats*

"SO, WHAT'S YOUR NAME?" THE young prince asked as he came apace. "Where're you from?"

"Amanita–" her voice cut off as if she was used to adding something after that. A surname perhaps? "And I'm not from around *here.*"

"I guessed *that,*" he said dryly, "seeing as I *know* everyone from *around here.*"

She was quite a bit darker-skinned than anyone from the valley-kingdoms, though he'd seen a few traders as dark as she. Her very dark brown hair had a reddish-cast to it where the sun must have stolen some of the color, so he could guess that she was an outdoorsy person – or at least that she'd been in the sun a lot as she traveled here. The hair was cut in a short, bushy bob that flounced a bit as she walked along with a sort of emphatic gait, making her look like a little kid, though he guessed she wasn't one.

"How old are you anyways?" Thony asked, as she didn't seem inclined to elaborate on where she *was* from.

"Thirteen. I think."

He looked at her askance. "How can you not *know?*"

She glowered up at him from beetled brows. "We count years differently where I'm from. I haven't bothered to sort out exactly how it all lines up and do the conversion." She muttered on in a low voice about someone named *'Quellarie'* saying it was *'close enough'*, but that part sounded more like she was talking to herself.

Amanita glared at him again. "Mr. Nosy, aren't you?"

Thony shrugged without taking umbrage. "I've found that nobody tells me the interesting things if I don't dig around a bit."

"Maybe they *would* if they didn't find you *nosing about.*"

He shrugged again. "That's been suggested before." By Joanna, actually. And Priscilla. "I tried it for awhile, but I just got blind-sided by a bunch of stuff."

By his *sisters* ditching him to go off on The bloody *Quest*. He'd forgiven them. Really, he had.

"Are your parents down in the village?" Thony tried again. "Or are they working in the castle now, too?" He hadn't heard of anyone new, but then he hadn't heard about *Amanita* either, so clearly he'd missed some things.

That startled a laugh out of her. "No. My mother is... an artist, I suppose. And my father used to herd sheep. Though only because *his* mother is the awfullest person *ever.*"

Thony blinked at that volunteered piece of information. "You, um, like your mother's mother better then?"

He had no particular preference or dislike for either set of *his* grandparents. He'd never met Grandpa Tom, of course, since Papa had inherited the throne before Priscilla had been born, let alone Thony, but Grandma Lizzy lived in the castle and was pretty sweet, though she was mostly bedridden now. Grandpa Dave and Grandma Marybeth visited a few times a year to compare *(and complain about)* grandchildren. Grandpa Dave had abdicated in favor of Mama's oldest brother, King Joe, even before Papa had been crowned. They were fairly mild people, much like Mama herself.

"Yes," Amanita sighed. "And no. She's... she has a lot of expectations. Of *me*. She..."

The girl stopped talking and shook her head sharply, as if she didn't want to explain any more.

She also looked a little baffled at the next cross-corridor. They'd hurried through these passages after the frog and apparently she wasn't all that familiar with the layout of the castle yet. Thony gestured to the right and she gave him a nod.

"So... brothers and sisters?" he asked as they turned.

She stopped suddenly, put her hands on her hips and glared at him again. "You really *are* Mr. Nosy-Pants today, aren't you?"

Thony put on his best, affected, 'Master Eswith' voice and said, "That's *Prince* Nosy-Pants to *you.*"

Apparently it was as silly as he had been shooting for, because after a brief, suspicious look, she giggled.

He grinned, dropping the voice, and said, "Actually, it's just Thony. And I'm only asking because you're clearly from somewhere else and that's *interesting*. And since you've probably seen by now that Aldyrwald is the most boring place on earth – on *any* earth," he added a bit sourly, and caught the surprised look she gave him, "so you can see why I'd want to know about anyone who's been somewhere more *interesting.*"

He really needed to not refer to other worlds. That the Fairy Wood led anywhere other than to the next valley over wasn't common knowledge *(plentiful fairytales notwithstanding).* Suggesting that it might would probably lead to a far less complimentary appellation than 'Affable' *or* 'Affirmative' being appended to his name. Not to mention that Prissy and the others had told him all about their adventures more or less in confidence.

She gave him a sympathetic look. "It's not that bad here, really. I used to think the same thing about... where I'm from. And after being a few other places you can see the way that home actually has a few things going for it."

"Besides family?" Thony sighed. "That might work for you, but I'm the *Heir* to the *Throne* and I'm never going to be allowed to go anywhere."

Amanita chewed her lip a little, and then clearly came to a decision. "Look, I came here – by myself – because I wanted to see what it was like without my family ordering me around all the time. So... I get it. And they're all nice people and all, but I don't want to talk about home. I want to try *this* place out."

"All right..." Thony sighed. She already seemed more interesting than anyone he'd met besides those occasional traders – and Mama had vapors if he tried talking to *them* very much. As if they were going to spirit him away in the night or something.

He could make a few guesses about Amanita already. She must be from very far away, with that dark complexion. And she must be from an honest-to-goodness *city* if her mother was an artist.

Uncle Louis, Papa's youngest brother who had gone away as a youngest prince was supposed to do and found a magickal cat and solved some riddles and ended up marrying a mermaid who turned out to be an enchanted princess, had sent them descriptions of *cities* on the coast. There were artists there, Uncle Louis had said, that stayed there all year long and for their whole lives, unlike the ones who visited Aldyrwald or the other valley-kingdoms for just long enough to fill all the local commissions before moving on. There wasn't enough business for even a single artist to stay on anywhere here, let alone to settle down and raise children.

Although she *had* said her father was a shepherd… so maybe he supported the family. Including her awful grandmother? And the grandmother with all the expectations?

Amanita gave him a friendly punch in the arm. "Besides, you owe me a frog. Unlike certain layabout princes, *I* have a *job* and I can't just go haring off to find another frog whenever I feel like it."

Which was sort of fair.

Thony was about to agree, but…

"What do you want a frog for anyways?"

There weren't a lot of innocent reasons for carrying a frog around in the castle. As he had reason to know.

"It's for a revenge prank," the girl told him seriously. "I'm supposed to be an apprentice pastry chef, not a scrubbing girl."

They had reached the scene of the spilled bucket. She only had the one floorbrush, so Thony headed off to a nearby broomcloset for mops. They worked together in silence for awhile. His curiosity about her was eating him up alive, but she'd asked him to respect her privacy, so… he'd have to find a more subtle approach. It might take a while.

"Thanks," Amanita said after a bit. "This is much easier with mops. And with help. And, actually, with the floor having had a chance to soak a bit. When they sent me up here the floor was so filthy that I thought maybe I'd fallen into one of those fairytales where you're given all these impossible tasks to complete in inadequate time and you have to befriend random talking animals to get it all done."

She paused thoughtfully in her mopping. "I suppose snatching the frog and keeping him in my pocket wasn't a great start on that if that had been the case. But he didn't *talk.*"

Well, according to Priscilla, humans were animals, too. Amanita had met Thony, and *he* talked. Though that didn't count in any fairytale he was familiar with.

Thony laughed. "I think that only happens if you're a princess-in-disguise or a poor miller's daughter. Why'd they only give you a scrub-brush anyways?"

The floor hadn't seemed that dirty to him, and he walked up and down this corridor several times a day.

"Part of the punishment, I assume," Amanita told him. "Though the Chief Cook didn't *say* I couldn't use a mop. I just didn't know where to find one." She looked down into the bucket. "This water is getting pretty filthy. I don't suppose there's anywhere we could dump it and get some fresh water?"

Thony looked into the bucket as well. The water looked okay to him, but... Presumably she just wanted to do a stellar job. He could understand. On those occasions when he'd been assigned to do chores to make up for some infraction or other, he'd wanted to do a really great job at it himself.

Of course, in *his* case, part of his motivation had been to be assigned to do *more* chores in the future, rather than more lessons.

"My rooms are just around the corner," he offered. "I have a bathtub that we could dump this in and refill it. We just have to be careful and not spill it in my bedroom on the way through." Which might be a bit of a problem... Maybe he should mention the servants' entrance to his bathroom, though that would be significantly out of the way... Was there a nearby guest-chamber that was uninhabited at present? He started going through in his head the various rooms nearby with attached baths.

Amanita leaned on her mop and gave him a skeptical look. "You want me to go in your rooms with you. Alone. In your *bed*room."

Thony rolled his eyes. "Don't try to make this sound like something it's not. I can go dump it myself and bring it back if you like. Maybe you *should* stay," he teased as he picked up the largely-refilled bucket. "The Chief Cook might come by to check on your progress."

As he'd guessed, that had her following him with alacrity. Not that it was likely; the Chief Cook was a busy man, so presumably the point of this punishment had been to get Amanita out of his kitchens and he really couldn't care less what happened to this hallway.

"Not likely," Amanita echoed his thoughts as she came up beside him and got a grip on the bucket's handle to take some of the weight from him. "But it doesn't really seem fair to make you carry this all on your lonesome."

"I think I could manage it," Thony said dryly, though he did set the bucket down to open the door to his rooms.

Such an endeavor required... care, after all. And he'd need to be able to see how much he'd have to do to make a path they could navigate with the bucket. He prided himself on having anything he could possibly ever need in there... somewhere. And since the only way to keep everyone from messing with his stuff had been to booby-trap the place, he'd done that years ago.

Innocuous things for the most part that left the invaders with oddly-colored hair or smelling weird. It hadn't taken long for the servants to realize that he was serious when he said he wanted privacy. It had taken rather longer for his *parents* to accept this – much to the dismay of the harried servants who had been required to enter his lair. Finally, Joanna had interceded, convincing King Bill and Queen Annabel that it was 'just a phase' and that they should leave him alone to 'grow out of it'. The compromise had been that he had to appear to be clean and decently dressed – including for formal dinners and such – and that there were to be no infestations.

It was... quieter than he'd expected on opening the door. Though he'd moved his traps in several feet a few years ago, for convenience's sake. And fortunately for this morning's situation, since if *Mama* had come away with blue hair, or smelling like the barrel of pickled herring Uncle Louis sent up every year as a 'gift', Thony suspected he'd be dealing with something rather more exotic than a few extra lessons with Master Eswith.

It was also rather *brighter* and *louder* than he'd left the place, generally preferring to keep the drapes drawn for a cave-like atmosphere. It was also helpful when he wanted to pretend to nefarious doings, not to mention that several of his on-going projects were somewhat sensitive...

He opened the door all the way and looked into a pristine bedroom. Not only were the drapes not drawn, but the light curtains behind them were billowing in a breeze that was coming in open windows – you could hear the usual mid-afternoon chatter and clatter of the main courtyard that his windows overlooked. The floor was swept – if not yet scrubbed. The bed was crisply made. The rugs were... *gone*, perhaps they were outside being beaten?

Amanita peered around him. "Hunh. Nice. I'd gotten the impression you were a total slob, but I guess not."

And with that expression of approval, Thony could hardly complain. Not that he knew her well enough to complain to. Why would she even care? *Years'* worth of projects...

He hefted his side of the bucket rather numbly and led her over to the bathroom.

That, at least, hadn't changed. But he'd been offered that he either had to keep the bathroom up to a hygienic standard on his own or the staff could service it via the second entrance. Thony had tried cleaning it himself for a month or so, then gratefully turned it back over to the professionals, trading cleanliness and freetime for a more minor invasion of his not-so-private-it-turned-out space. He'd left his dirty clothes and sheets in here as well, and the staff would collect them and leave him fresh items, even installing a hanging rack and shelves, though it had been made clear to him that the items were to be removed to storage in his proper wardrobes and chests of drawers, a crown prince's collection of clothing neither fitting in a smallish bathroom nor being likely to stand up well to humidity.

They dumped the bucket together, being careful not to splash their half-dried clothing. Amanita decided to run back out for the mops and brush and rinse them as well after a look at the ring of grime in the tub left from dumping the bucket. Thony was instructed to rinse the bucket *several* times before refilling it.

He did so mechanically, his mind running in circles of benumbed horror at his losses.

She was back after a few minutes; stopping in his bedroom to talk to someone he noticed absently.

"Good job," the girl said, inspecting the bucket critically after putting brush and mops in the tub. So apparently, he could rinse a bucket to the satisfaction of an apprentice pastry chef/neat nut. Yay. "You have a guest waiting for you."

Thony went out into his bedroom.

To his entire lack of surprise, it was Joanna. She was sitting on the bed – the *perfectly-made* bed that was wearing a crisp new coverlet that he'd never seen before – the burgeoning curve of her pregnant belly belling out her gown more than he was used to, and patted the spot beside her. He came and sat down, still feeling almost too overwhelmed for tears, let alone words.

Joanna settled an arm around his shoulders.

"I tried to save what I could identify as a 'project'," his eldest sister said gently, gesturing at shelves that he hadn't even gotten around to noticing were now neatly packed with a dense array of his stuff. "I didn't find out what Papa had gotten started in here until I had Mama settled and Prissy came by to tell me." She paused. "You... had to know what would happen when Mama got a peek in here."

"It... must have been fast work," he choked out. "I guess I didn't do as good a job at booby-trapping the place as I thought."

He might have caught a glimpse of a wince out of the corner of his eye. He heard an uncomfortable chuckle. "Really, it's more like gold is more powerful than the fear of having green hair for awhile. Papa paid everyone *really*, really well, I hear. I think they just tripped the traps... but from the chatter I heard they might even be grateful to you for giving them a chance to earn such a large bonus. Though white vinegar might be a bit dear in the village market for awhile until all the smells and colors have gone away."

There was a faint scent of vinegar, Thony realized. That was probably why the windows had been left open.

He supposed he should be relieved that the servants weren't going to be angry at him.

"And... my rats?" he asked, trying to keep the tears out of his voice.

"Prissy took them, of course," Joanna said gently. "She... was rather more impressed with your sense of compassion than anyone else was inclined to be." Anyone else... apparently included Joanna. "*I* rather thought that if you could spend all that time training them to avoid traps, you could train them to avoid the castle altogether." Far easier said than done. The rats were interested in the things he'd been doing with them, but avoiding abundant sources of food and nesting material – not so much.

"And then there was Mama, of course," Joanna was adding. "Since the agreement had been that there weren't to be any infestations–"

"They *weren't* an infestation!" Thony exclaimed indignantly. "I was training them – we were creating a *circus*, like in the storybooks..." Something else he'd never seen for real, because no self-respecting circus would waste its time traveling among all these little mountain villages.

Joanna sighed. "Maybe if it hadn't been Mama who saw them first, sweetie. Or if they hadn't all fled into every nook and cranny as soon as she opened the door."

The way he'd taught them... which was also part of their nature...

"So, she didn't get to see any of their tricks, then?" he half-asked sadly.

"I don't think it would have mattered," his sister's tone was still gentle. "You know how Mama is about rodents."

Indeed. Mama had had vapors every year until Thony had been too old for the Springtime Bunny to leave him baskets of treats. He'd heard that the Bunny still visited the younger servants and pages, leaving bunny-trails of colorful eggs to help them find the sweets and baskets of newly hatched chicks and ducklings, but everyone was careful to keep Mama from finding out. Queen Annabel thought it was adorable to see the children with a line of chicks or ducklings following behind them, but she managed to put it out of her head where those little creatures had come from. It might be why she didn't accept younger girls for her ladies-in-waiting, though.

And bunnies weren't even properly rodents – though Thony could sort of see her point, given how *large* the Springtime Bunny was purported to be.

Down in the village, he'd seen that baby *bunnies* were included in the Springtime baskets.

Of course, the reason they needed all those baby fowl and bunnies each year was because the previous year's batch had been eaten, once they were big enough. It was enough to make Thony slightly relieved that *he'd* never been left any live creatures to make pets of before they became dinner and he wasn't quite sure how the other children had managed it.

Mama was alright with kittens and puppies.

Not frogs, though.

"Thony..." Joanna said quietly, "Papa says the servants are to come in to clean regularly now."

They might as well. All his work was lost...

"And it's never to return to that state."

No chance to *rebuild...?*

"What am I supposed to *do*, then, Jo?" the young prince asked, a little desperately. "I'm still riding the same tired old pony I had when I was eight – not that I'm allowed to ride him anywhere. I'm not allowed to learn to use a sword or a bow or even how to start a fire, so Gods know... hmmn..." he eyed her askance, then shook his head and went on, "*who* knows how I'm going to manage if I ever *do* get to go anywhere. I know as much mathematics as our Minister of the Treasury – not that it's all that much, since our tax system and budget are really *not* that complex." His hands had clenched, and he forced them to open again on his thighs before his short nails cut crescents into his palms. "I know all the geography for the mountain region – and I'm never going to be allowed to do so much as go over to the next valley-kingdom, so really what's the point in learning what's beyond *that*? History? I know *ours* back for five hundred years, and again, *no one cares.*"

Joanna sighed. "There's always more to learn – as I'm discovering – but... I can see what you mean. At some point you won't have anyone to stop you, but..."

When Papa *died* and Thony was crowned king.

"But then I'll have *responsibilities* to keep me from going anywhere."

Not to mention that, even if Papa was a little ditzy and overprotective, Thony loved him dearly and didn't look forward to that day. He looked down and didn't stop his hands from curling into fists again.

"You'll... need to find a bride," Joanna offered reluctantly. She knew that was the last thing he cared about right now, but it *was* a way for him to get out of the valley. Traditionally, a prince who was going to be a king would find his bride out in the wilderness. And given Priscilla's tail – and the fears of the surrounding royalty about that Bad Blood – it would likely be some worthy miller's daughter, not a princess languishing in a tower.

And *those* stories always ended up with the *miller's daughter* having adventures to win the *prince*... Not the other way around.

"Hey, Prince Nosy-Pants, are you coming back out, or shall I finish up on my own?" Amanita asked. She was balancing both mops and the brush in addition to the bucket and Thony leapt up to give her a hand.

"I'll... see what I can do," Joanna offered. And she – or rather She, he still hadn't gotten used to that yet – was offering him the Word of a Goddess. Not that even as a Goddess would Joanna interfere more than slightly. And She was far more likely to use her persuasive skills on their parents than anything more... exotic. But... he didn't need to doubt that *something* would change.

He nodded his thanks and followed Amanita back out to the significantly less dirty hallway.

"Not looking forwards to finding your fairytale princess?" Amanita asked after they were mopping again, so apparently she'd heard the tail end of his conversation with Joanna.

Thony shrugged. His sisters' transformation into honest-to-goodness Goddesses wasn't common knowledge yet outside of Aldyrwald – and never mind the mountain that had sprung up and enveloped the back half of the castle when the Ragnarök took place. It was the Holy Place of Earth, it had been explained to him and it was for that as much as anything to do with family that Joanna had stayed here. Roger was God of Air, and there was apparently a perpetual and unmoving tornado somewhere on the opposite side of the world *(where Thony would never get to see it)* and he had to spend a certain amount of time there, but the rest of it he spent here with Joanna, pretending they were just a normal young couple expecting their first child.

But Priscilla's tail was hardly a secret.

"The other royals in the surrounding valley-kingdoms all think we have Bad Blood," he explained with as much casualness as he could. "And they're all kind of jerks anyways. So, I'd have to go pretty far to find someone and that is *clearly* not happening, since Mama and Papa won't let me out of sight of the castle. So, it'll have to be a worthy miller's daughter for me, I suppose. Not that I'd *want* to marry any of those *princesses,*" he added in an aggressive mutter, "no sense of humor and no compassion. Just like their brothers. And their parents." He wouldn't add 'and dumb as rocks', though, *honestly?*

Amanita nodded as if all of that made perfect sense to her. "All these little pocket nations. They either have to spend all their energies snubbing each other over tea or they go to war and conquer each other. Kind of sucks when you're the one getting snubbed, though."

Thony decided to focus on the part that wasn't so sympathetic it made him want to wince. "Well, we sorted the conquering part out several hundred years ago and no one even has standing armies anymore, so that's out. Just a few handfuls of knights-errant to deal with ogres and giants and robbers and the like. I guess they do things differently where you're from?"

"*Very,*" was the dry reply. "Aren't any of you worried about an outside force coming in to conquer all your little fertile valleys?"

He shrugged again. "Aldyrwald is pretty central. And the mountains themselves are defenses of a sort."

"*Some,*" Amanita said with feeling. "Not enough against a determined invader if you don't have *people* to defend all those mountain passes and all."

"We have a resident Goddess," Thony noted, thinking about how Joanna was the least war-like person ever.

"That didn't help *my* people," Amanita told him directly. Then she aggressively pumped her mop up and down in the bucket and wrung it out a little more vigorously than necessary. They were trying to mop water *off* the floor now. "But that was thousands of years ago. And really, *really* far away. I just think you shouldn't get too complacent. These little valley-kingdoms of yours are peaceful and prosperous. That's an attractive combination to... some people."

He gave her an alarmed look. "Did you see or hear something on your way here?"

She shook her head quickly. "No. I'm just familiar with the problem. For historical reasons. And... I kind of like it here. I'd hate to see this place wrecked."

"Um." Thony didn't know what he could do about this. He'd considered the problem a few times over the years, but the peace in the valley-kingdoms was more fragile than it looked. It was more of a *détente*, actually. If one country started to make any sort of efforts towards building a credible defense force, the ones around it – for two out in every direction, at least – would take that as a threat. A country out on the edges of the region – where there tended to be more robbers and it was necessary to keep a few more knights around to protect the caravan routes – *might* be able to do something like that without destabilizing the whole region. But Aldyrwald in the very center – not a chance. They hadn't even had *robbers* in the mountains around Aldyrwald's three connected valleys since at least Thony's great-grandfather's reign.

"So, um, what was it you did to irritate the Chief Cook enough to get floor scrubbing as a punishment?" he asked after a moment, deciding a change of subject was in order.

Amanita sighed heavily. "It was *totally* not my fault. This other guy? the *journeyman* pastry chef? He started getting grabby, using *my* set of equipment after he'd gotten *his* all dirty and not even asking or cleaning it up and putting it away or anything." She gave Thony a frank look. "I hate it when people mess with *my* stuff, too."

Well. That was an acknowledgment of what he'd just gone through. Thony nodded in appreciation.

"So, what did you do?" he asked. "And does this have something to do with why there wasn't any dessert last night?"

King Bill had been... displeased.

Amanita snickered. "I switched the salt and sugar. In my *own* containers, I'll note. If Mr. Grabby-Hands hadn't taken my stuff, there wouldn't have been any trouble at all. Or if they'd let me make the after-dinner dessert in the first place, since *my* stuff was all sparkling clean and shiny." Thony could bet it was, given how she'd gone after the floor. "And since we sample everything before we send it upstairs, His Majesty – and all y'all – didn't get a super-salty cake or anything."

Thony grinned. This was the kind of prank he could appreciate wholeheartedly. "Seems like this shouldn't have gotten *you* in trouble though."

She gave him a nod with a tilted head and raised brows. "I know, right? But this guy – the journeyman pastry chef, his name is *Paul* – so *Paul* decides it's all my fault and he's going to tattle on me."

Thony frowned. "It still seems like this is his fault for not taking better care of his own equipment."

He knew Paul slightly, of course, and had to admit the young man was not one of *his* favorite people either. Nor was the Chief Cook, honestly, though he respected the man's ability to put excellent meals on the royal table at regular intervals, as well as feed the entire staff. When King Bill didn't get fed on a regular schedule, he tended to get... loud. And Queen Annabel tended to faint more than usual.

Hmmn. Perhaps he should make sure Mama had had all her teas and things today. All things considered.

And the *staff* not getting fed didn't bear thinking about.

"See, that's what *I* thought. But *Paul* decided to sabotage the replacement dessert I was working on and I caught him doing it, and we ended up having a food-fight with half the cooks taking sides and the other half hiding under the tables. It wasn't a big deal except for the mess," the girl added nonchalantly. "Dinner was all upstairs by then and the dishwashers were just waiting for the plates and platters to be brought back down. Since there wasn't a dessert to go *up*, given that *Paul* had ruined both his *and* mine by that point. But the Chief Cook got it into his head that this was all *my* fault. So. Here I am."

She gestured at the sparkling, clean hallway.

Thony leaned on his mop. "Well, I can say that this hallway has never looked better. So, what's up with the frog?"

"I'm getting *Paul* back of course," Amanita said with a surprised look. She gave the bucket and the recumbent floorbrush a disdainful sniff. "I mean, what *else* can they do to me?"

Well. They could fire her.

Though... not if Thony could help it. He didn't have so many friends that he was willing to give up even such a new one

Being Heir to the Throne should come in handy for *something* occasionally, shouldn't it?

"Looks like the floor is pretty much done," he said as casually as he could manage.

"Where did the mops come from?" Amanita asked. "I think you said it was a closet? We should probably make sure they dry before they go back in and make the place all smelly."

"There's a place they dry mops down near the kitchen," Thony told her. "I'll help you carry everything down."

She gave him a narrow-eyed look. "Because I need a big, strong *boy* to help me carry stuff?"

He rolled his eyes. "Hardly. Though I think we can both agree that it's easier to carry the bucket with two people. It's just a lot of stuff. And the kitchens are a far ways to go."

She gave him a level look. "That's not it, though, is it?"

What was it about girls? Or – not *girls*, since most of his mother's ladies-in-waiting were silly as a flock of geese and the village and servant girls were hardly any better. This Amanita had that same look Joanna did when she knew he was Up To Something. Even Priscilla got that expression occasionally... though in the Good Old Days Prissy had often been helping him out with the Something.

"The Chief Cook isn't a big one on second chances," Thony admitted. He knew *that* all too well for himself. "I don't want him to fire you for what wasn't even your fault."

Amanita's eyes softened somewhat. "That's very... gentlemanly of you. But I can handle this on my own. I *need* to handle this on my own. That's the whole point."

The whole point of *what*, she didn't say, but he supposed he could guess. Being on her own, tiny as she was, and not always relying on a family that would bail her out of anything and everything.

"You're not likely to get to be a pastry cook again," he warned.

She sniffed. "Like I'd want to work with *Paul.*"

"All right," he sighed.

She gave him a buoying smile. "Here. You take the mops and dry them out somewhere. I can manage the brush and the bucket, but the mops... are a bit much. You're right."

Not to mention that she'd have to explain where she'd gotten the mops. And why she had two of them. And how Queen Annabel had fainted again would probably come up... Thony realized Amanita had kept behind him and stayed in the shadows when the ladies-in-waiting might have seen her.

He accepted the brooms and she gave him a jaunty nod and hoisted brush and bucket. "See you around, Prince Nosy-Pants."

"See you around, Princess Too-Clever-For-Your-Own-Good," he threw back. She shot him a suspicious glance over her shoulder, then grinned. And headed off.

Thony sighed and hoisted the not-quite dripping mops.

Where to let them dry?

Well, the windows to his room *were* open now...

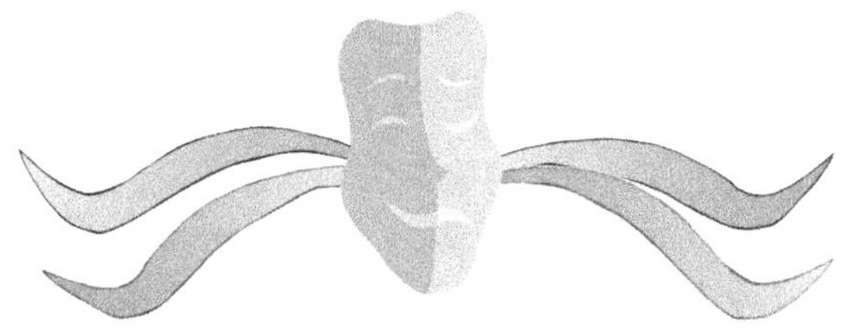

Chapter THREE

Some Improvements *(But Not Much)*

True to Joanna's word, some changes appeared in Thony's life.

He was allowed to bid his tired old pony fare-thee-well and see the old fellow put out to pasture. The pony was too aged even to serve as a first mount for the more timid new pages or ladies-in-waiting. Which said something right there.

Thony's new mount was a full-sized mare... though nearly as old as the pony and about as spirited as a plowhorse. However, it was *(literally)* a step up in the world, and Thony spent a fair amount of time in the stables making friends with Rosie.

This, too, was a relatively new experience. He knew where the stables *were*, of course, but always before his pony had been brought out to him, saddled and tacked up to practice in the riding salle under the riding master's bored eye. Sometimes he'd even been allowed to take a few turns around a fenced-in meadow that was just a few acres too large to be called a pasture. *(Or so he was told. Thony failed to appreciate the difference.)* When he was done, the pony had been guided away by a stableboy.

(Thony had once campaigned to be able to make up for some infraction by doing what he had read was heavy labor in the stables. Even Joanna had laughed at that idea, noting that they weren't such idiots as to give him access to that much raw material.)

Now he was permitted to enter the stables and shown how to saddle and bridle his own horse. And how to brush her down afterwards and put out water and fresh oats. Apparently, *someone* had decided that he might have matured a bit.

He still wasn't invited to *clean* Rosie's stall, and his tentative hints that he'd like to help were ignored. He had to wonder whether there were still some lingering concerns about what he might do with his access to the stables. Though that might have been as much because he was a prince and the thought of watching him shovel 'stable-sweepings' made at least some of the older grooms and stablehands uncomfortable.

The younger ones as well – at least in the sense that they were terribly polite and tried to stay out of his sight as much as possible.

And Thony discovered that it bothered him. At least a bit.

He was, by nature, mostly a loner, but he'd been rather *extremely* alone since his sisters had left on The Quest and come back so changed.

His father's pages and squires had never been interested in befriending him – those who were eldest-born and destined to be his future vassals seemed intent on impressing him with their skills *(i.e., showing off)*, the middle-borns were vaguely resentful, and the handful of youngest-born lucky-numbered boys *(the ones who weren't being kept at home to be properly ignored and vilified so as to make them more worthy of a truly fairytale ending)* had their eyes on the future and were completely uninterested in him. Thony had tried hanging out with them anyways, but since the only classes they shared in common were the boring ones – since he wasn't being allowed to learn to use sword or bow – and since they were kept fairly busy with the non-boring ones, it hadn't worked out all that well.

Not that he could blame the boys. A tighter connection with the royal family was always beneficial to the first-borns *(as the future lords of their small demesnes)*. And the last-borns had better things to do with their time as they imagined and prepared for their Great Futures.

And as for the middle-borns... His own five uncles on his father's side – the ones younger than King Bill and older than Uncle Louis – were all knights-errant and stopped by on occasion to visit. They all had a vaguely miserable and desperate look to them – as did Mama's one middle-born brother on the rare occasions he dropped by. Papa always told them they were welcome to stay, but – aside from the occasional Winter when options were thin on the slopes – they preferred not to live off of his charity. *(Thony wasn't sure why staying in Aldyrwald and serving the duties of a knight for his father counted as 'charity' as opposed to doing the same on a short-term contract for some other valley-kingdom. But his uncles certainly seemed to think it made a difference and since it was their lives, it wasn't really Thony's place to disagree.)*

Mama's ladies-in-waiting were even worse. Because of the Devinthals' supposed Bad Blood, it was possible that this would be the once-in-a-generation opportunity for a noblemaiden from one of the lesser families to marry into royalty. Usually princes – the ones who *counted* as decent husband material because they were Heir to the Throne or the youngest-born – married princesses. Or at least worthy miller's daughters. But the kings of the surrounding valley-kingdoms seemed vastly uninterested – not even inviting the Devinthals to their own children's sixteenth birthday galas – and the offspring of the local millers in Aldyrwald's three valleys had all run to boys. *(There were some miller's daughters who were toddlers now, and a handful who were close to twice Thony's age... and married... with batches of children of their own...)*

So, every time Queen Annabel's ladies saw Thony it was *awkward.* First, they'd all look at him with those doe-eyed, hopeful looks *(and he was well aware that they practiced those looks in the mirror for hours at a time – he'd watched the older girls do that when he was small and played around their feet in his mother's solarium after all).* Then the *tittering* behind their hands would start as soon as he actually started talking to Mama or anyone.

It was... uncomfortable to say the least. Thony didn't want to give any of the ladies-in-waiting the Wrong Idea, and he wasn't entirely sure what he might do *(or not do)* to cause that to happen. So – once he'd gotten old enough that they stopped treating him like a somewhat feral pet and started treating him like a prize to be captured – the young prince had started avoiding them as much as he could.

Unfortunately, this had meant avoiding Mama a fair amount as well, but such was life. Though when Prissy and Joanna had spent most of their days in the solarium also, it had truly been a sacrifice.

His other options for finding friends had been among the younger staff of the castle or the village children. But the former tended to be busy and somewhat leery that he might get them involved in his pranks, and it was hard to get to know the latter when he was *strongly discouraged* from going down to the village. *(Such discouragement taking the form of unexplained additional lessons with Master Eswith, writing letters for Mama, boring the riding master – Great-Uncle Sir Eddie, a retired knight who was King Bill's uncle – to tears by trying to persuade the old pony into doing something resembling dressage, or other things that were time-consuming and ultimately useless.)*

The stables had been an area he hadn't explored thoroughly in the past, having been warned off by Great-Uncle Sir Eddie not even to try anything. *(Great-Uncle Sir Eddie had no sense of humor and a great deal of patience, but little interest in doing more than the minimum required as a riding master. Not that there was a great deal to be done when all Thony had been allowed was the pony. And Rosie clearly wasn't much of a step up in the eyes of a man who had once jousted on the back of a fiery-eyed charger.)*

The boys in the stables *(and it seemed to be uniformly boys, though exactly why, Thony wasn't sure)* seemed to have a great deal more freetime than the servants in the castle. Stablemaster Thaddeus had a fair amount of tolerance and permitted a great deal of goofing off so long as the work got done, the equines in his care were healthy and happy, and no one took the joshing past a certain line that seemed to have more to do with safety than anything else. When one of the lads got too much hay stuffed down his pants or something and hurt feelings ensued, the stablemaster would make sure that the victim was all right... and then take the perpetrator off for a quiet talk. None of the boys so talked to seemed particularly squished afterwards, though they almost invariably apologized for whatever it was they had done, shook hands, and went back to work with a will.

Thony had figured most of this out by watching discreetly while he tended his horse, or from somewhat unobvious watching posts. He wasn't trying to *spy* on them, after all. Just... imagine what it might be like to be part of their group.

Though he'd apparently earned the trust – or at least sympathy – of the stablemaster. He would often give the young prince a gentle clap on the back as the older man passed him by in one of those unobtrusive watching posts, or say a few words of encouragement. Which was more than Great-Uncle Sir Eddie had ever bothered with.

It... wasn't ideal, but it was a definite improvement and Thony restrained his impulses to liven things up in favor of not losing these modest new privileges.

His self-control seemed to bear fruit after a couple of weeks when he was permitted to go on first accompanied, and finally *solitary*, rides into the carefully groomed miniature *forest* just beyond the village. It was still located in the center of the valley-bottom, and served more to provide a divider between villages and a place where the bounty of the forest – wild nuts and berries, truffles for the pigs and such – might be harvested than a real wilderness.

But it was *Out* of *Sight* of the castle!

Who knew where such insane recklessness might take him? Perhaps the next time King Bill made a jaunt in a carriage over to one of the other connected valleys that he ruled, he might take Thony with him. *(Oh, be still his beating heart!)*

This... *extended glade*, it might be more fair to call it than an actual *woods*, was on the opposite side of the castle from the notorious Fairy Wood that his sisters had disappeared into for The Quest. A place that even *they* agreed was as dodgy and dangerous as Thony could dream of and Mama could fear.

There was no possible way the young prince could get from the one to the other without being spotted, even if he should manage to convince his sleepy mare to move at something resembling a trot. Even if he actually wanted to.

Which he didn't. For all his aversion to the Immense and Stultifying Boringness of Aldyrwald and his yearning for adventures, Thony was still a responsible and thoughtful young man. He didn't really want to terrify his parents and risk his life for nothing more than to alleviate his boredom... he *was* the Heir to the Throne after all, and there really wasn't anyone else to take it, now that Joanna and Priscilla were both out of the running for having the kingdom as their dowry. One of his knighted uncles *could*, possibly, but they had neither the training nor experience and at this point were kind of old; even Uncle Louis, who had married the enchanted princess and now waited as her prince-consort to eventually rule her father's kingdom by the sea, was over *thirty*. Not that Uncle Louis needed a second kingdom to rule.

So, for now, Thony sated his restless spirit by riding obediently into the tame little glen, dismounting to whack at trees with sticks for awhile in imitation of the pages and squires, and then riding obediently back to the stables. Once there he would take care of his horse, watch the stableboys for awhile, then head back up to the castle-proper for meals and protocol lessons.

It wasn't great, but it was an improvement and... well, he'd take what he could get.

Occasionally he wandered by the kitchens to see if that new girl, Amanita, was free. Unfortunately, she never *was*, but he was at least able to verify that she'd kept her job, albeit as a dishwasher. She seemed to be doing the smart thing and keeping her nose down – no more pranks, even to take vengeance on the journeyman pastry chef – and successfully staying out of the Chief Cook's sights.

Hanging around waiting for her to be free was another sort of thing that could give people the Wrong Idea, and, since she was clearly neither a miller's daughter nor a princess-in-disguise, people having the Wrong Idea would cause the girl no end of trouble. Reluctantly, he settled for knowing she hadn't lost her job and he gave up on finding further chances to quiz her about the places she'd been.

After several days of riding alone into the mini-forest, Thony reined up sharply as he came across another rider, cloaked and looking unreasonably mysterious for the center of Aldyrwald.

"Ho, there, Thony," the rider called and threw back his hood.

It was Roger. One of the young prince's favorite people... and better yet, he'd brought a pair of wooden practice-swords.

Over the next week, Roger *(who was actually Prince Sir Roger, having served as page and squire here in Aldyrwald and then returned home to be knighted by his father, King Richie)* introduced Thony to the beginnings of swordwork. After several days more, he added some basic lessons in archery.

And several days after *that*, they were joined by Priscilla's husband, Jeremy. The young male centaur told Thony, with a cheerful disdain, to ignore everything Roger had told him about the bow. Archery was apparently a specialty of centaurs, and he took over Thony's lessons in that area – though, unlike Roger, he couldn't demonstrate the proper stance with his horse legs.

The pair of easygoing young men *(or rather God and centaur stallion)* seemed to enjoy Thony's company – and each other's – as much as he did theirs. Occasionally they would face off with the wooden swords themselves to demonstrate a point, and Thony would watch their skill with not-so-secret glee. Neither one was foolish enough to suggest trying edged steel – the ring of weapon against weapon would surely out their little lessons if they did, the glen being located where it was between the two villages.

It was no particular mystery that no village girls out berrying or boys driving pigs were ever out there to *see* them engaged in these unapproved practice sessions; Thony's parents likely had sent out some sort of edict to stay out of that bit of forest in the mornings. He had no idea why Mama was so insistent he not spend time with the villagers – unless she had some insane notion that he'd 'fall in love' with someone other than an enchanted princess or worthy miller's daughter... or at least a well-connected noblemaiden.

As *if*.

In Thony's opinion the whole reason for the existence of princesses *(and miller's daughters)* was to provide an excuse for princes to go on adventures *(well, except for his sisters)*. Having to marry the rescued princess was sort of the price you had to pay for having the adventures.

Thony had no idea if there was a point to his brothers-in-law's help *(and <u>Roger's</u> Divine help, in particular. He was aware that he was improving faster than an hour or so a day could account for, and with no chance to practice on his own)*. For now, he was content to merely have more to do than before to fill his days. And to hope that, if he ever *did* end up getting sent off into the somewhat less-well-maintained wilderness on the upper slopes of the mountains surrounding Aldyrwald to find his bride, he wouldn't be a total loser and not even know how to properly unsheathe his blade *(not that they'd covered unsheathing blades yet, given that they were sticking to wood)*.

That was an obvious route to ending up with the *miller's daughter* rescuing Thony instead of *him* rescuing a languishing *princess*.

Not that Thony had anything *against* miller's daughters. In fact, he'd far rather find one of them than marry one of the awful princesses who had so ruined first Joanna's and then

Priscilla's sixteenth birthdays. And he was more than grateful that neither of his sisters would be relegated to having to marry one of the princesses' just-as-awful brothers.

The sixteenth birthday was, of course, the all-important one. That was when a prince or princess – or a commoner – was first eligible to marry. Boys often waited a little longer – earning their shields, starting businesses, or waiting to be crowned king. But for girls, sixteen was the proper age.

The *magickal* age. The age at which fairies and witches and ogres and giants were most interested in them and therefore most likely to set the girl on the path to a fairytale ending.

Not that every one of them – even the lucky-numbered ones – found such an ending.

It often took a fair amount of effort on the part of royal parents to arrange for an evil spell to be cast, a giant or ogre to be willing to risk life and limb to rescuing princes, and so on. Not to mention that there were only one or two kings with the wherewithal for a truly impressive setup like a mountain made of glass.

(The king who had scrimped and saved to have that monstrosity created had made back his original investment several times over, renting the place out to other kings so their daughters could languish properly. Though Thony had heard a rumor that all that money just barely covered upkeep, since a mountain made of glass was bound to require a certain amount of regular repairs and glassmakers weren't cheap. Not to mention the expense of keeping the whole thing shined – because, seriously? who would want to 'imprison' their daughter on a smudged or dusty mountain? And what self-respecting prince would bother attempting to scale a glass mountain that didn't sparkle fit to blind them?

Thony had occasionally wondered if the creator had planned for sanitary facilities on the top and whether the resident princess', ah, bathwater could be seen flowing down... And then there would be the entire logistical nightmare of getting food and water – and the princess – up to the top in the first place. Not that he'd be likely to get a chance to find out how it all worked for himself – the glass mountain was three kingdoms to the east and was almost certainly out of King Bill's reach for arranging Thony's future princess to be stashed on.)

It was the Done Thing to have a birthday gala for the newly eligible prince or princess, and invite all the royalty – and a significant portion of the lesser nobility – from all the valley-kingdoms for two out in every direction. There was no question but that this was an opportunity for the kings and queens to look over their potential sons- and daughters-in-law and for the bolder of those young people to attempt some efforts at courting. If the pairings they found for themselves were acceptable in the eyes of the parents, they *might*, after all, even find their rescuer-rescuee situation being setup to make it permanent.

Joanna's birthday bash had, however, been a disaster.

Thony had been only five, but he could still remember some of the other royal children – apparently having heard about Prissy's tail – harassing his sweet, golden-haired sister until she cried and her tail snuck out from under her skirts. And then they'd pulled it and laughed at her. *(Thony had gotten them all back with some help from the younger staff of the castle, though it had done their relations with the other royals no good and it had taken days to track down all the frogs. That had also been the end of any chance he'd had of befriending the Chief Cook.)*

While he had run off to find frogs for his revenge pranks, Joanna had quietly and firmly shooed away seven-year-old Priscilla's tormentors. She'd then politely and just as firmly berated the visiting royal parents for not instilling better manners in their offspring and departed the party to put Priscilla to bed. She hadn't returned.

That had not improved relations with their neighbors either.

Joanna had received neither proposals of marriage nor requests to arrange for her to languish somewhere. And Roger's visits had been curtailed for awhile... though only for a *little* while – he'd still been one of King Bill's squires then, after all. And even Roger hadn't dared to flout his royal parents and ask her to marry him on his own recognizance. *Then.*

Priscilla's party had gone, if anything, even worse.

Mama had insisted she tie that problematic tail to her leg, binding it securely, despite the fact that Priscilla transformed from energetic and delightful to sad and quiet when they tried this. Not to mention that they had never yet discovered a method of binding down the tail that worked past something occurring that excited or upset Thony's sensitive sister. Under normal circumstances she simply threaded it through holes in her specially-designed gowns; it seemed somehow more than merely *wrong* not to see the glossy shine of that black fur, the happy curl at the tip, or Prissy's fingers fidgeting with the long, almost-prehensile – and definitely expressive – length.

But Joanna was twenty-five then and behind her Wise and Wonderful patience there rested a look of resignation. There hadn't been much chance that *she* would see offers of marriage at that age, so she was destined to be a Princess-Aunt to Thony's future children. *(And no matter that Prince Roger from the valley-kingdom next-door had stuck around to visit back and forth, unlike every other middle-born knighted prince in the area. He hadn't proposed, despite what was clear to see in his eyes, nor spoken of love as far as Thony had ever heard. More than once, he'd seen Joanna stand atop one of the turrets to watch Roger ride away home until his tiny form had vanished entirely... and then turn away with her usual, imperturbable expression and eyes that were entirely too bright.)*

If, however, Priscilla's classical beauty and sunny disposition – and the visual absence of her tail – could be made to overcome rumor and innuendo... perhaps *she* at least might find a husband.

Thony could have told them it wouldn't work.

Prissy's anxiety over the whole affair, coupled with testing, taunting comments by their royal peers, had worked her into a State, as Mama put it. The tail came free, there was a collective gasp of gleeful horror that made it clear that their guests had been here for a show rather than to examine her as a potential bride or daughter-in-law.

Priscilla had fled again, weeping.

Thony had cast a dark look around the room *(memorizing every face, though he later collected a copy of the guest-list also)* and then followed after her to her room. She'd locked the door, but he could hear her crying. Thony could easily pick the lock *(that was actually a service he performed for the castle, since Mama often lost the keys to important places like the pantry)*, but he doubted that would help, so he kept knocking, pleading with her to let him in.

Joanna had arrived, trailed as always by Roger. And she had somehow persuaded Priscilla to open the door. They'd all gone in to try to soothe the younger princess...

...and somehow the result of that had been that the girls had left that very night – with Roger going along to protect them – on The Quest. Thony had been detailed to remain at home to provide sufficient distractions to give them a head start. No one had mentioned explicitly that the Heir to the Throne couldn't vanish so easily. *(It hadn't occurred to him till later that the whole thing fell together too quickly. Clearly Joanna had been planning something like this for awhile... And how had Thony never figured that out ahead of time?)*

It had been to his utter dismay to discover that hardly any effort at distraction was needed at all. He wouldn't go so far as to say that his parents were relieved at the disappearance of their problematic daughters, but they were certainly... *sanguine* about it. Thony didn't doubt that Queen Annabel and King Bill *loved* Joanna and Priscilla, but he overheard them discussing how this might make it easier to marry *him* off if the neighbors could only be persuaded to forget about the older girls.

Not that it mattered to *him*. Thony had decided that night that he would *die* before he married anyone from that group of thoughtless, hateful jerks.

He hadn't mentioned that to anyone, though. Mama and Papa seemed anxious enough without him making Dire Proclamations.

He suspected that Joanna might have picked up on the idea, however, based on the way he referred to anyone from the neighboring valley-kingdoms, other than Roger's family. *(Not that Roger's parents had let him court and propose to Joanna until it was out of their control either, but at least they had been better about everything. And they hadn't caused a fuss when presented with the done deal.)* It was possible that these lessons with Roger and Jeremy were a way of helping him prepare for his own Quest in the far-off someday when he'd have to go at least *three* kingdoms out to find a princess-bride.

His far, *far*, FAR-off future.

And nevermind the disturbing snippets he kept overhearing from his parents.

If King Bill and Queen Annabel could ignore things they didn't like until the bothersome stuff went away – and actually make that *work* – surely it would work for Thony, too. Right?

In the meantime, at least, the young prince was getting to know Jeremy, getting to spend time with Roger *(whom he'd always admired)*, and learning some useful skills. Even without him going out of his way to make it happen, life was a little more interesting.

He could live with that.

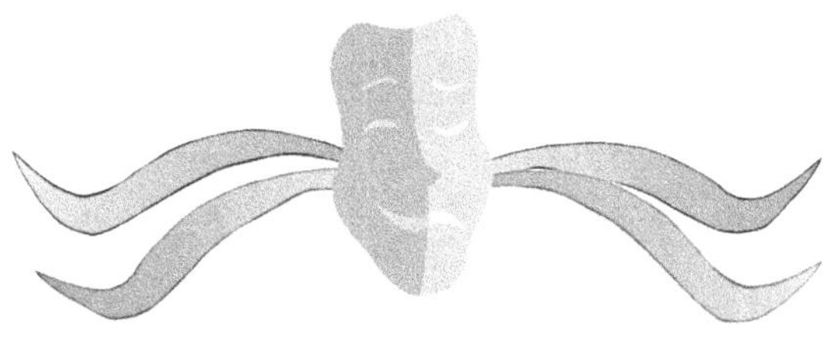

Chapter FOUR

The, er, *Accident*

THE FIRST INDICATION SOMETHING WAS wrong was the sounds of the awful row coming up from the kitchens. Thony could hear it through the open windows of Mama's solarium as he was subjected to the newest incarnation of the horrors of protocol – though for once it was at Queen Annabel's direction, and not Master Eswith's, nor even as a punishment handed down by King Bill.

Mama had decided Thony needed to learn how to dance.

Or rather how to learn to dance *better*, since he'd learned to dance at Prissy's side, having always been close in height to her despite her nearly two years of greater age. That had been great fun, and they'd both ended up being more than passable at the variety of steps and styles popular in the valley-kingdoms.

The last time he'd had to brush up his skills had been some ten months ago for Prissy's party, so he'd thought he'd be good for at least another year. Mama was chalking this new torture up to a number of new dances having become fashionable – and she'd even hired a dance-master from outside of Aldyrwald. Since they hadn't yet covered anything Thony wasn't already familiar with in a week of torment, the young prince was doing his level-best to ignore the implications as hard as he possibly could.

It wouldn't be so awful if he could have done this with Priscilla. Or Joanna. Or even *Mama*, now that he'd maybe begun on that growth spurt and was nearly as tall as she or Joanna were. He didn't mind *dancing*, especially compared to other incarnations of those infernal and infinite protocol lessons. Anything that got one moving around was worthwhile, in his opinion, and his sense of timing was superb *(even if he did say so himself)*. The dance-master wasn't too horrible, and the musicians were of the quality one might expect in the royal castle of a very tiny kingdom: good, but not spectacular. They played at most of the castle's dinners and events, and better ones were only brought in for such grand affairs as weddings and funerals... and sixteenth birthday marriage markets.

No, the problem was that Prissy and Jo were busy doing Goddess-Stuff, and Mama was pleading a bad knee *(that Thony had never heard of before, so he was somewhat suspicious)*.

Which left... the ladies-in-waiting.

And swirling *them* around the solarium under the dance-master's direction was likely to result in *someone* getting the Wrong Idea.

So when the sounds of shouting and slamming of ladles on pots *(or at least something that sounded awfully a lot like that)* caught Thony's attention, he was very relieved to hear Mama say, "Whatever can be the problem? Someone, please go check."

Unfortunately that was followed immediately by "Not you, Thony dear. You'll likely only add to the chaos. And you have a lesson to finish."

"Yes, Mama," he said with a sigh and went back to the task of dancing his latest partner around the solarium and listening to a steady stream of things like:

"Your Highness, you must *look* at your dancing partner while you dance."

"Don't hold her like she's something *slimy*, Thony dear."

"Your feet know what they are doing, Your Highness. Please reserve your eyes for your partner."

And so on.

He manfully refrained from pointing out that he'd much more enthusiastically hold a 'slimy' frog than one of the ladies-in-waiting, and fixed his eyes on the girl's left eyebrow. She was a little taller than him, and he knew better than to look straight ahead in *that* situation.

But when the musicians halted – mid-measure and the girl stumbled a little, though Thony had been through enough reprimands about that not to do the same – so that the returned lady-in-waiting could report to Queen Annabel, he was altogether ready to stop.

"The Chief Cook is in a *terrible* mood, ma'am," the young woman – this one closer to Joanna's age and not so much 'waiting' anymore – curtsied politely. "I'm not sure if dinner will make it to the table. The place is a mess, and he's shouting and sending people off."

Thony didn't stop to hear if there was anymore – he was out the door as soon as he heard the words 'sending people off' and was around two corners and out of earshot before Mama could think to call him back. There were a number of people who might fall under the Chief Cook's vexation, but if it was the one he guessed...

Thony skirted the kitchens after the briefest peek to get a sense of the situation. Regardless of what his mother thought, he knew better than to enter a situation that contained chaos not of his own making. Also, the Chief Cook still had it in for him for things he'd done when he was seven or eight *(or five)* years old.

He knew where the servants' quarters were, though not which room might belong to that mysterious, dark-skinned girl who had refused to tell him where she came from. Not that he needed directions when only one door on the corridor was open and there were sniffly, growly sounds coming from it.

Amanita looked like she might have grown an inch or so in the last month as well. It left her merely small for her age instead of verging on tiny.

She was packing – if you could call it that. Slamming personal items into a duffel-bag with fervor and... remarkably clean foul-language. Thony wasn't all that familiar with swear-words himself, Aldyrwald being as boring as it was, but he guessed he could identify them if they ever came in range of his ears. And these weren't. Even the ones in another language that she lapsed into out of frustration every now and then were somehow clearly... pretty tame.

He arranged himself in the doorframe, leaning back with folded arms and trying to look worldly-wise before coming to her attention.

"So, what happened?" he asked.

Amanita whirled around, glaring, saw who it was, and turned back to her 'packing'.

"I've been fired. And it wasn't even my *fault*. It was an *accident.*"

Thony nodded to himself. He'd thought it might be something like that. Once you were on the Chief Cook's bad side, any little thing... "Would this *accident* happen to have involved Paul?"

She snorted, though it sounded a little wavery. "*Him.* He's not worth the effort."

Okay, then.

"What are you going to do?" the young prince asked.

She shrugged, dumping all her possessions back out on her bed when the duffel's ties failed to come anywhere near closing it.

"I don't know. Go somewhere else. *Not* back home. Not... yet anyways. I think." She began re-folding the clothing with unnecessarily meticulousness and packing them carefully so everything would fit. It wasn't actually all that much; it was just that the bag was pretty small.

"Can you tell me what *did* happen? I might have an idea or two," Thony prodded. "Was it a prank gone wrong?"

"No. Yes." She sat down on the cot that had been hers until this last hour with a thump. "Do you know that guy, David? He thinks he''s King of the Soup or something. The Chief Cook keeps going on about how he's some kind of stew-making *genius.*"

"I know him," Thony admitted. David was a few months younger than him, and the Chief Cook's son. As such he had some sort of rank amongst the commoners as well as more or less unlimited access to the sweets and treats generated in the kitchen. While his dad wasn't much on second-chances for anyone *else*, David could do no wrong in his eyes.

He was pretty spoiled, with a sense of entitlement a mile long *(which was honestly pretty impressive if the Only Son of the king noticed; Joanna and Priscilla had done a pretty good job of keeping Thony's ego in check, but he was aware he probably didn't notice how much he took for granted).* David wasn't necessarily a bad sort otherwise and had made himself a reputation for generosity by sharing out his plunder with the other children in the castle... even occasionally including a certain crown prince. But everyone knew better than to cross him anywhere near his father's domain.

"He's a jerk," Amanita said succinctly.

Thony shrugged noncommittally. "All right. What did he do?"

"He..." She looked at her clenched fists with a grim expression as her cheeks turned red.

Oh, no. This could be bad. David's sense of entitlement extended to everything – and every*one* – that could be construed as belonging to the kitchens. This might be more than merely giving Amanita a hand. This might be something Thony would have to bring to his father's attention. And hopefully *not* have to point out to King Bill that a spectacular Chief Cook was *not* worth keeping on if his son was abusing people.

"Did he... hurt you?" Thony asked with some alarm.

Amanita looked up in surprise, the blush fading a bit. "What? No. As *if*. He... got fresh with me, I suppose you could put it. He got me alone in the dish-pantry while I was putting stuff away – you know I've been on dishwashing duty since I was demoted from apprentice pastry chef...?"

Thony nodded, and she went on.

"Yeah, well, it's boring, but it's work and I'm doing something useful. I'm beginning to see what you mean about Aldyrwald, though working as a dishwasher probably isn't the best way to assess that. Anyways, he got me alone in the dish pantry and tried to kiss me."

"Tried and *failed*, I assume?" Thony wasn't really less alarmed yet.

She shrugged. "Well, yeah. *Obviously*. And I didn't have to give him a fat lip or anything." Amanita gnawed a bit on her own lip. "He... sort of implied he wasn't done with *trying*, though."

The young prince relaxed minutely. It sounded like she was getting away before a real problem occurred. Though he'd have to somehow keep an eye on the kitchens from now on, unless David was only targeting Amanita because she didn't have her own people – and as far as he knew, everyone else *did*. "Did you tell the Chief Cook or something? Is that how you got fired?"

The girl shook her head, short bushy hair bouncing a bit. "No. I know the Cook is his dad, so that wasn't going to get me anywhere. He wasn't going to be able to *hurt* me," Amanita assured the prince. "I know how to take care of myself. *I* traveled with an Iana warrior for the first couple of months when I left home."

It sounded like she was boasting, but Thony had never heard of Iana warriors and gave her a blank look.

She rolled her eyes. "I also had a bunch of training *before* leaving home. Since I was a real little kid. All right? Mr. 'Make the Stew' dude isn't going to keep a hand on me without my permission. Not that he'd *get* my permission," she added darkly. "As *if.*"

There was clearly still a missing piece of the story.

"So... you didn't hit David," Thony summarized. "And you didn't report him. And he didn't hurt you – not that he *could* have," he rolled his eyes as she gave him a sharp look. David stood a good head-and-a-half taller than her and was probably close to twice her weight. He... reserved the right to be skeptical of the tiny girl's claims. "But you still got fired. What gives?"

Amanita sighed. “I figured that I didn’t want *dude* to sneak up on me in the dark or something. I’d *have* to hurt him to get away then, and I figured that wouldn't go over real well. So... I decided to teach him not to mess with me.”

Thony raised an inquiring eyebrow.

“I was going to put a couple of frogs in his stew,” she admitted.

“That doesn’t really sound like an accident,” the prince pointed out.

She shrugged. “One of the frogs got out of my pocket while I was going over to the stew-pot David was assembling, and while I was trying to discreetly retrieve it, I slipped on something and knocked the pot over.”

Thony could envision the mess – spiced water and vegetables and browned meat everywhere, the frogs hopping around, *ribbeting*.

“And... the pot kind of *catapulted,*” Amanita elaborated. “And it... kind of flung all its contents. Um. Into the Chief Cook’s face.”

Thony’s imagination added a Chief Cook dripping spiced water and with wilted parsley dangling from his ear.

“That... would do it...” he commented faintly.

It was a... *glory* of a mess, to be sure.

“It was an *accident,*” Amanita said again, looking at him as if she wanted at least one person to believe her.

“Um,” Thony said. This might be described as many things, but he wasn’t actually sure *‘accident’* was one of them. And he was sort of an expert in pranks gone wrong and the results thereof.

Her chin dropped. "And *Paul* just stood there *laughing* his *head* off. So, I think he may at least be on probation.So, at least something good came out of this, I suppose."

Thony sighed, and came in to stuff the last few items in her duffel-bag.

"Come with me," he said, hoisting her bag onto one shoulder and tugging her along with his other hand.

It said worlds about how shaken she was that she didn't even object to him carrying the bag, let alone telling her what to do.

He took her to the stables, of course. Stablemaster Thaddeus would be a much better fit as her supervisor than the humorless Chief Cook. Amanita would be the only girl, but Thony had the feeling that was more by tradition than for any reason that the stablemaster would care about. And the prince rather suspected that this girl would be the answer to a problem that had been plaguing the stables since his sisters came back from The Quest.

He was right. Thaddeus quizzed her on a few things – including the debacle that had gotten her dismissed from the kitchens. His blue-grey eyes sparkled with amusement as he stroked his short, full beard, and at last he nodded. One of the grooms was summoned to assign her a sleeping space, put her on the chore roster, and show her around.

"That was a kind thing to do, Your Highness," the stablemaster said, looking after her with a thoughtful expression. Amanita had perked right up now that she had a Plan and a Place and she was energetically asking the groom about everything. She was also at least passingly familiar with stables, and already seemed more comfortable here than she had been in the kitchens.

Thony shrugged a little awkwardly. "Well, we're supposed to keep an eye on Our People and solve problems for them, after all. Kind of my job." He gave Thaddeus a direct look. "And I thought she might be helpful with Twinklestar."

The stablemaster's clear gaze swiveled to fasten on him. "There's some as wouldn't do so. Some as feel it's beneath them."

"Not *here,*" Thony averred. "Maybe the royal jerks in the surrounding kingdoms, but not here."

Was that really true, though? *He* certainly didn't see helping the People as beneath him. Nor would Priscilla or Joanna. Even before the whole God Thing happened, they had both spent a fair amount of time doing just that. And Roger was the same.

Mama and Papa though... he was ashamed to say he couldn't say for sure. And Great-Uncle Sir Eddie...? Highly unlikely.

"Hmmn." Stablemaster Thaddeus surveyed him for a moment. "Seems like you've grown a bit, Your Highness."

"It's just Thony," the prince said absently as he tried to discreetly check his cuffs. *He'd* thought he might have started that growth spurt Prissy had been promising him, but last he'd been able to tell, all his clothes still fit the same so he'd been guessing it was wishful thinking.

The man chuckled. "Then I'm just Tad. I think you'll be needing a new saddle."

Thony looked up from trying to see if his ankles were showing more than his wrists. "A saddle?"

Tad nodded. "That one there would be a good fit." He indicated a saddle setup in the nearby mending area for some minor repair. "Thing is, a saddle for a horse is like a pair of boots for a man." He lifted a booted foot and wiggled the toes. "They mold themselves to fit the wearer. You can't wear another man's boots without getting blisters, and a horse can't wear another's saddle."

The young prince frowned in confusion.

"That saddle belongs to Silverfoot, there," the stablemaster pointed his beard at an alert-looking dapple-grey a few stalls this side of the nearly somnolent Rosie. " 'M afraid you'll have to take the horse along with the saddle."

Thony blinked in surprise. He'd thought... no, he'd been *sure* that King Bill had laid down a series of parameters along the lines of which horses Thony might be permitted to *touch*, let alone ride. And surely Silverfoot – who had noticed the attention and was meeting his gaze while Rosie dozed, nose in her manger – was the antithesis of any of those parameters. He didn't want Tad to get in trouble with Papa...

But, oh! he *did* want to ride that horse.

The kind stablemaster apparently saw his indecision.

"His Highness, Sir Edward, has been complaining that he can't teach you anything new, even now that you've been riding Rosie," Tad commented. "He'll be pleased to see you on a different mount."

His Highness, Sir Edward? Oh. Great-Uncle Sir Eddie. Thony tended to forget the man was also a prince of the Realm, but he was a middle-born brother of Thony's deceased grandfather, King Tom.

"Do you really...?" The young prince wanted to ask if Tad really thought this could work, but he was having trouble taking his eyes off the beautiful horse.

"I'm sure His Highness will be pleased to tell your father how much progress you can make on a proper steed," Tad suggested. "Since it was His Highness' *own idea*, after all. He's certainly expressed his opinion that you need a better horse if you're to learn anything more from him. *Frequently.*"

There was a certain dry amusement to that last comment. Doubtless the stablemaster had been the recipient of the elderly knight's diatribes on the matter as often as Thony had.

Thony tore his eyes from the really cool horse to look at the man. It *might* work. Great-Uncle Sir Eddie could often be 'persuaded' to do things if he thought they were his own idea. And he was one of the few people in Aldyrwald whom King Bill treated with a measure of deference; out of respect for his grey hairs, presumably.

"I... guess I could ride Silverfoot," Thony said slowly. "Since I need a new saddle. And since it wouldn't be kind to the horses to switch them. As you said." His eyes were being drawn back to the dapple-grey and his hands twitched to touch that soft nose and give the gelding a good scratch... and saddle him up and try out his paces.

The stablemaster chuckled and clapped him on the back. "Go make friends with him, lad. You might want to take him out in the practice arena for a few turns while you get to know each other. Before you take him out to the forest."

"I'll do that..." Thony was fishing in his pocket for the apples he always stashed before coming down here, but this had been an unplanned excursion. Tad snatched his hand and dumped a handful of sugar cubes into it, closing the boy's fingers over them, all without Thony looking. Another clap on the back got him started towards the horse.

His horse. And one that was already pointing his ears towards Thony in curiosity... while Rosie didn't even twitch at the approach of her erstwhile rider.

This was going to be a *very* good day.

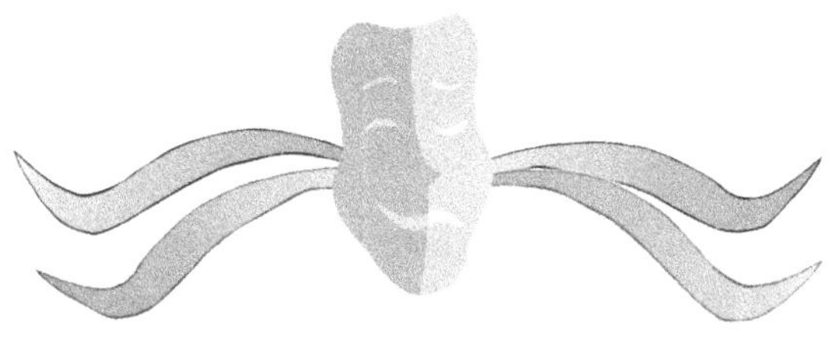

Chapter FIVE

Somebody Had to Do It

AMANITA SETTLING IN TO THE stables meant some changes for Thony. Good ones, all.

It took a week or so, of course.

The older stablehands and grooms took to the energetic and curious girl quickly, ignoring her gender once she'd switched her kitchen-girl's skirts for a stableboy's shirt and trews. She was eager to learn, worked hard at whatever task was put to her and took corrections seriously and without undue drama. They really couldn't ask for much else.

The stable*boys*, however, had a somewhat different take on the whole thing.

First of all, Amanita was tiny. The stables didn't hire on help until a boy was at least twelve and usually not until they'd gotten enough growth on that the stablemaster felt it unlikely that the horses would step on them by accident. It took some doing to establish that she was nearly at *(or perhaps slightly past)* her fourteenth birthday. That she just came from shorter people, and wasn't expecting to grow terribly tall, even as an adult. Also, that she was familiar enough with horses and stables that she wasn't likely to get stepped on.

The second problem was that she was a *girl.* Their reaction there seemed to be less about the actual fact of her gender than that this had meant she got a private room like one of the adult stablehands, rather than bunking up in the hayloft like the rest of the boys, with only a locker-box to keep their private items in. Since he'd seen her wistful look at the loft... and the airless hole of a cleared-out closet that was her 'room', Thony knew she'd rather be out there with the boys but was too sensible to raise a complaint. As with David in the kitchens, the young prince realized that commoners could get the Wrong Idea as much as ladies-in-waiting – he knew that the staff and villagers occasionally married as early as fifteen, but clearly Amanita wasn't concerned about becoming an Old Maid.

Though she, at least, would have useful skills to trade for a living, unlike his mother's ladies, unless you counted embroidery.

Though, arguably, that *was* earning a few of them a living. The ones who were long past the ages when they were likely to find a husband, but continued to stay on in the castle, running his mother's errands, writing out her letters for her, and keeping her entertained. *(Well, writing her letters when Thony wasn't assigned to do that as a punishment and his sisters weren't available. Queen Annabel felt it was her Moral Duty to write to her parents weekly and her nine older brothers and sisters each at least monthly, but she rather loathed putting pen to paper. She wasn't terribly fond of reading, either, and would often have someone read the responses to her. One of her ladies' other duties was reading aloud stories and poetry to the entire gaggle of noblewomen, though Queen Annabel would frequently sigh reminiscently about the Good Old Days when*

King Bill was wooing her and would read poetry to her himself. Not poetry he'd written himself, mostly, probably for good reason. Thony had seen what a mess his father could make of Royal Edicts – he shuddered to imagine what Papa's attempts at poetry might sound like.)

Since Thony had a perfectly valid reason to be in the stables a couple of times a day *(unlike the kitchens)* he was able to keep tabs on Amanita's progress.

About the only thing the stableboys *didn't* resent her for was how she had taken over care of the unicorn who had followed Priscilla back from The Quest.

Twinklestar had moved himself into the stables, demanding – via Prissy's interpretation – a loose-box that let onto a lush pasture. In return, he blessed the castle's water sources with purity and kept all the other equines in the stables generally healthy. Possibly the stable*hands* as well; he hadn't been clear on that, and since they were generally a healthy bunch it was a little hard to tell for sure.

Unfortunately, Twinklestar wasn't on the best terms with Priscilla right now.

He had apparently chosen her as his unicorn-maiden *before* the whole Goddess Thing happened and felt he had dibs on her. Since unicorn-*maidens* had certain very specific requirements and Priscilla was now married to Jeremy and really didn't meet those requirements, this had caused a number of hard feelings on Twinklestar's part. The fact that one of Priscilla's Aspects was Goddess of Love didn't seem to convince the unicorn that Things Had Changed. (*Presiding over what was euphemistically called 'Love' was apparently a facet of being Goddess of Animals, she had explained to Thony without the slightest hint of a blush. She had changed a great deal from the girl who would blush prettily in perfect princessly manner at pretty much anything. This time he'd had to stop her from explaining far more than he really wanted to know about this.)*

The result was that Twinklestar had become very *grumpy* and *particular* about who cleaned his stall and refilled his oats and water. He was intelligent enough that the stall didn't get all that dirty, but he liked the hay to be fluffed and refilled at regular intervals. And with his long, shining, and very fine mane and tail, the unicorn really needed a human to groom him.

Twinklestar being *grumpy* and *particular*, however, translated into the unicorn insisting on thoroughly sniffing anyone who came near him and threatening anyone who didn't meet his particular standard. And just being sniffed by a large creature with a very pointy horn – Twinklestar was the size of a rather tall pony, not a horse, but still – was pretty darned intimidating. And if his stall was tended, while he was out in the pasture, by someone who *didn't* meet his standard, the unicorn would throw a hissy fit and upset all the other equines for a day and a night.

Not to mention that none of the adult grooms met his standard. And none of the older stableboys wanted to *admit* that they met his standard, so they refused to go near him. And the younger boys wanted to emulate the older ones, so *they* had to be coerced into performing the necessary chores as well.

Priscilla came by as often as she could manage to groom him, but then they tended to get into arguments which sounded very strange and one-sided, since Twinklestar spoke only telepathically.

Fortunately, Amanita got along with Twinklestar like peas and carrots. She didn't understand him, she said, but she clearly had some form of communication with the irritable equine. In casual conversation with Thony, she let drop that she'd had contact with other unicorns – or at least *an* other unicorn – in the past.

*Un*fortunately, not having to deal with the temperamental Twinklestar didn't sufficiently mitigate the resentment of the boys.

Thony had been keeping an eye on the situation as best he could – he knew that Tad and the older stablehands were as well, of course – but it all came to a head one day just before he arrived for his daily ride.

One of the boys – Wesley, a lad who was close to Thony's age, but somewhat larger in most dimensions – gave the small girl a hearty shove face-first into a pile of stable-sweepings that she'd just collected from several stalls. This particular stableboy wasn't usually such a huge idiot, in the young prince's opinion, but not only did he do the dirty deed, but he then stood there watching as she extracted herself from the mess.

What neither Wes, nor the other boys who had gathered around to laugh, was expecting was how quickly Amanita would recover. She'd somehow managed to avoid the more liquidy parts herself, but she came back up fast with two handfuls of the goo and leapt onto Wes, rubbing it into his hair. And then stuffed a load of *clean* straw into the back of his pants, just for good measure.

When Thony arrived – moments after Tad, it appeared – the stablemaster was giving out a great belly-laugh.

The young prince was waved on ahead to saddle his horse. He kept sneaking peeks back down the aisle, much to Silverfoot's annoyance – to keep an eye on the proceedings. Amanita was given an amused, but firm talking to and sent off to clean up. Wes looked like he would be given the same treatment as Thony led his horse out of the barn.

Roger wasn't in the forest for his lesson today, so it was entirely archery with Jeremy.

The handsome young centaur was the son (or colt) of the leaders of the centaur herd that had followed his sisters and Roger out of the Fairy Wood. Mariah and Caspar, his parents, had decided that their herd could use the adventure of a world that had never known centaur hoofbeats before... but the decision had been spurred on by their son falling in love with Priscilla. Exactly how it would all pan out in the end was still a question – centaurs had *very* long lifespans by comparison to humans, but in the end, Jeremy was still mortal and Priscilla... *wasn't*. Not to mention the much more near-term problem that King Bill and Queen Annabel refused to acknowledge the existence of their second son-in-law and Priscilla's attempts to bring them around generally went about as well as her visits to Twinklestar.

And for much the same reason.

Thony wondered occasionally whether his parents would be *more* or *less* horrified to know that Priscilla used her Goddess-Powers to turn into a centauress when she was out running with the herd... and Jeremy. Prissy wasn't sure either and wasn't willing to test the question, so she'd sworn her brother to secrecy.

And oddly, through all of this, Queen Annabel had developed a cordial relationship with Mariah that had her having tea prepared in the cherry orchard at least twice a week so that Jeremy's mother could attend. And King Bill had gone shooting with Caspar and some of his huntsmen and Caspar's stallions and was planning another hunt.

For his own part, Thony thought Jeremy was just as cool as Roger. He'd have been happy to learn archery from *anyone* who was willing to work with him, but Jeremy made the whole thing a complete hoot. They usually spent the whole time laughing and joking while Jeremy thought up more and more exotic and elaborate targets for Thony to attempt. *Jeremy* could make any shot he tried, of course, but *Thony's* attempts often resulted in... well, *hilarity* was both accurate and kind.

If Roger had always been the much older brother Thony didn't have, Jeremy was the only slightly older brother he'd never had either. If Jeremy didn't go all goo-goo-eyed every time Priscilla's name came up, Thony would happily have named him his second-best friend. *(I mean, really, he probably was, but that was just... awkward.)*

Today, though, Thony updated the stallion on the Amanita situation and the pair of them mulled over the weirdness of *girls* and *boys* and *people in general.* Jeremy, it turned out, was getting some pushback from the fillies in his herd for having chosen a human over one of *them*. Shape-shifting Goddess or not. He had been in more or less the same position as Thony – expected to follow his sire as herd-stallion and with all the fillies trying to flirt with him from *far* before he was even *close* to being interested. He admitted, readily, that he'd found Prissy interesting at first simply because she *wasn't* trying to vamp him. It was something even Roger didn't really understand, being a middle-born son and not the Heir.

And the craziest part of the thing was actually that the herd-*mare* usually chose the herd-stallion, just like with wild horses. The positions were usually settled via competitions of various sorts – tests of strength and athletic ability for the stallions, and tests of wisdom and endurance for the mares. So, there was no *rational* reason to expect Jeremy to end up as herd-stallion after his father... but since he had no sisters, the fillies had decided for him, or so they'd thought.

"I'll get it sorted out... eventually," Jeremy said with a sigh. "It helps when Pris is there with me. No one actually considers challenging a Goddess in Her Presence. But... She has a fair number of other responsibilities. She's said I can go with her, but my Dam and Sire say they need my help while the herd settles in..."

Thony gave him an understanding nod. He knew that Caspar and Mariah *liked* Priscilla, but that they were worried about the likely longevity of the relationship on their son's behalf. *They* acknowledged that the pair were married – or mated – but male centaurs weren't usually monogamous, so they saw no reason to help rein in the fillies and their ambitions. It was... a lot to sort out. And Jeremy tagging along after Priscilla on Her Goddess-Duties could all too easily end with him feeling like a second tail.

There wasn't much the young prince could do other than be sympathetic, though. And tell Jeremy funny stories about Priscilla from before The Quest.

He returned to the barn after his secret lesson – and before Great-Uncle Sir Eddie would show up for a riding 'lesson'. *(Tad's subterfuge had worked spectacularly and Great-Uncle Sir Eddie had adopted Thony's switch in mounts as if it were entirely his idea. His 'lessons' were proceeding much more quickly now, though that was as much due to what Jeremy and Roger were teaching him about horsemanship as anything the elderly 'riding master' was doing.)*

Wes was still washing his hair at the pump. He helped Thony rotate the faucet back into position to fill the trough for Silverfoot to drink, then Thony helped him push it back out of the way to rinse off what Wes said ruefully was the *third* wash.

"How is it?" the bigger boy asked after his hair was no longer sudsy.

Thony took a careful sniff. "Maybe one more time." Or two, but no point in getting ahead of themselves.

Wes sighed, and began rubbing soap into his hair again.

"So, why'd you do it?" Thony asked as he watched and his horse drank his fill. It wasn't so warm a day, nor had he taken the gelding at any speed, so the young prince didn't need to be careful to control how much his horse drank. "I'm sure I've heard you telling the others that she wasn't such a bad sort and they should lay off of her."

Wesley shrugged. "If it wasn't me it was going to be someone else. And probably someone with more of an axe to grind over her being here. But now it's done. She's shown she can give as good as she gets – and that she's willing to laugh it off afterwards. We shook hands between washes two and three," he explained.

Thony nodded. That all seemed reasonable. "You know she's probably still going to feel like she needs to get you back for having started it, right?"

Another shrug. "I'm a big boy. I can take a prank or two. So long as she doesn't flip out if I prank her back."

Oh, this was a kid after his own heart. Thony grinned at him. "I think you can be pretty sure of that–"

He stopped speaking as he saw Great-Uncle Sir Eddie approach the horse trough.

"There you are, young man." It was hard to tell if his great-uncle/riding master was *actually* smelling the faint aroma of dung that still clung to Wes; he *always* looked like he was in the presence of a bad smell. "You have returned from your little morning jaunt, I see. Worn off some of that unnecessary exuberance, I hope." The man also never actually asked questions when he could make rhetorical statements suffice.

"Yes, sir, I hope so, too," Thony replied politely. "Are you ready to start? I think Silverfoot has had enough of a drink."

"Indeed. I believe a groom will be bringing forth my steed any moment now." Great-Uncle Sir Eddie pointedly averted his eyes from Wes, who was vigorously scrubbing at his scalp. "Her Majesty asked me to remind you to be certain that you *bathe* before your dance lesson this afternoon. *I* would request that you find a less... public venue to do so. Bathing," he added pointedly, "should be a *private* affair."

Thony rather seriously doubted that Mama had asked Great-Uncle Sir Eddie to say any such thing. It would be totally out of character for Mama. Not to mention that he always *did*, and this made it sound like bathing was something Thony had to be cajoled into doing.

He was about to respond a bit tartly – though it was likely to get him in trouble, it wasn't fair for a member of the royal family to be so rude to a commoner – but Wes caught his eye. Since Great-Uncle Sir Eddie was insistently *not* noticing him, he had stepped a little farther out of sight and was now prancing around with his nose in the air and pretending to scrub himself all over. Thony had to bite his lip to hold in a guffaw.

"Yes, sir," he said meekly instead as Wes winked at him and Tad himself brought the riding master's properly caparisoned horse out to him.

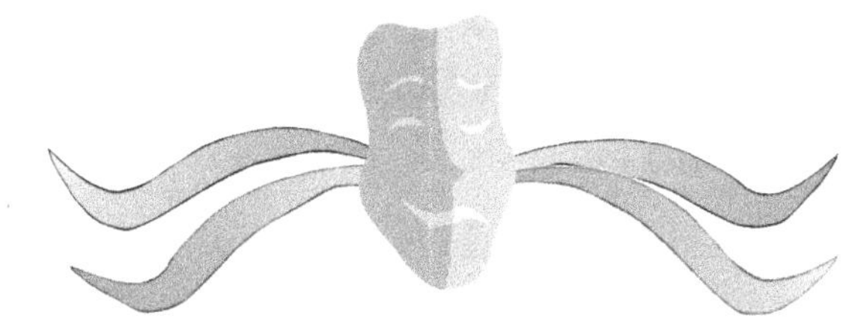

Chapter SIX

The "Rewards" of "Virtue"

IT TOOK LESS THAN ANOTHER full week for Thony to become fast friends with Wesley – and Amanita. The three of them shared a sense of humor, and Wes shared Thony's curiosity about the rest of the world outside Aldyrwald. Between the two of them, they were able to peel a few tidbits off of Amanita.

Apparently, the country she was from *(that she still wouldn't name, though she claimed it was because there was zero chance they'd ever heard of it, so there was no point)* was matriarchal. Wes had never heard the term before, and Thony had needed to think for a moment to make it make sense for him as well. Or at least to comprehend the meaning. It still didn't make *sense.*

(I mean, seriously? Girls running an entire country? He supposed he could imagine Joanna – or even Priscilla – doing that. But that was two girls out of the tens of thousands that a country would hold. And all the other ones were silly geese that he'd met so far.)

She'd given him a *look* when he said some of that aloud and told him rather pointedly that the *women* had thrown an invading force from a culture of tall, *patriarchal* types out.

Thony would believe *that* when he saw some independent corroboration.

Wes, it turned out, had agreed with him, but he'd been clever enough to keep his mouth shut when Thony and Amanita had started to get into it.

"No wonder she worries about us getting invaded," Wes commented when the two boys were talking later. "If her whole country is filled up with short little women who are trying to run things, they probably have to deal with that all the time. Poor little things."

"Hmmn," Thony had replied. Wesley didn't seem to see the corollary to his statement, which was that if Amanita's people were constantly under threat of invasion those tiny little women must have gotten pretty good at repelling invaders. Or else they hired mercenaries to do it for them. And what were their men doing while the women were running things? She'd said her father herded sheep.

She'd also mentioned that she'd traveled for awhile before settling in Aldyrwald, and since Amanita was only just shy of fourteen, that was something to think about right there.

She'd said her family was loving and supportive – except for her hag of a grandmother. And she seemed not to want to talk about them too much, though whether that was from homesickness or a sense of guilt that she had people left behind who would be worrying, he couldn't tell. She *did* sort of imply that there was some sort of deadline – a time limit before she *had* to go home and face up to those family expectations and responsibilities.

The look on Amanita's face when she said that... was probably the look Thony wore when he thought about his own future.

It felt, for no particular reason he could name, like she was someone who would understand his own ambivalence and guilt and sense of responsibility. Like Jeremy.

It also felt, however, like Wes and Amanita were becoming much closer friends with each other than either one was with him.

That was probably to be expected, Thony supposed. They worked together, ate together, and had next-to-unlimited time to prank each other or to work out pranks to try on the other stableboys; fighting with Wes and showing she could be a good sport afterwards had done her a solid with the other boys. That, and Wes was a favorite with everyone, despite or, perhaps, because of his good-natured pranking about, and he had sort of nominated himself as her sponsor – meaning that anyone who wanted to mess with *her* had to go through Wes as well. And *he* had a pack of buddies he could call on. Not that Tad let things build up like that anyways.

Thony, by contrast, was only in the stables a couple hours a day. Any pranks they pulled on *him* needed to fit into that time frame *(and risk coming under Great-Uncle Sir Eddie's disapproving eye)* or they needed to find an excuse to go up to the castle. And vice versa. He was happy to have a couple of casual friends – which was a couple more than he'd had before – but... well, it was what it was.

While most of their 'unnecessary exuberance', as Great-Uncle Sir Eddie had called it, was now absorbed in a never-ending series of pranks directed at each other, they were also working out some plots to try on other people. It was nice to have multiple minds going over a plan to look for flaws.

The target they were working up to was David.

While Amanita had sort of agreed that the, er, *accident* that had gotten her fired from the kitchens had probably been more her fault than anything, they all agreed that David needed to be taught a lesson about respecting other people's personal space. Unfortunately, David rarely left his father's demesne, and that meant coming up with a plan that would both leave the desired impression and not seriously impede the usual work of the staff. Thony had flatly refused to be a part of anything that resulted in King Bill not getting fed on time.

The complexity of the endeavor meant a great many planning sessions, but since that was at least half the fun, none of them minded.

And the rest of the denizens of stables and barn breathed a silent, collective sigh of relief as the tricksy trio's attentions were absorbed in theory rather than *practicum*.

Thony was strolling down a corridor in the castle on his way back to his rooms for a shower before his daily dancing lesson, mulling over their latest potential scheme, when he heard voices coming from what his mother liked to call her 'office'.

"– enough *time*, dear." Queen Annabel's voice was verging on querulous.

"This is just a first pass, sweetheart," King Bill replied.

Papa was in there with her? Thony whisked himself into an embrasure behind a potted plant. He'd long ago discovered that this particular embrasure had a crack at a convenient height that went straight through the wall into his mother's 'office'. It funneled sound right to the ear of anyone standing by it, but the potted plant made them almost entirely invisible. *(Persuading the staff that this particular, huge specimen belonged here had actually been the hardest part. And, unfortunately, once he'd gotten that accomplished, he'd had to face the grim truth that Mama's office was where all other boredom went to die. Of boredom. And now, the one time something interesting might be going on in there they left the door open so anyone could hear what they were saying without any special effort whatsoever. Though hearing them* <u>*without*</u> *being detected might be a different story. And was why Thony was behind the plant.)*

He'd clearly missed something while paying attention to getting situated.

"– like you haven't known about this," King Bill was saying a little impatiently. "We've been discussing this ever since the girls came home. And you've had those dancing lessons going on for nearly a month. Whyfor if not for this?"

"It gives us all something to *do,*" Queen Annabel sighed. *Mama* was bored? "We used to go to balls and fairs and tourneys in the other countries fairly regularly, Bill. You remember." She sighed again, a little petulantly. "It wouldn't be such a hassle if Joanna could help me write out all the invitations. You know I hate to do that. And she's always so *busy* nowadays."

King Bill *harumphed* as he always did when they brushed up against the edges of the changes in their daughters. "Have some of your ladies-in-waiting write them out for you then."

"You wanted this to stay a secret as long as possible," she replied a little tartly. "If I bring any of *them* into this, Word will be out across all the valleys faster than the invitations are sent. Though there's a limitation to how long we can keep this under wraps anyways. The staff will have to be told so they can plan ahead for all the guests."

Guests... Invitations... *Dancing* lessons... There was only one possible reason they would be hosting such an event...

"I have faith in you, sweetheart," Papa replied. "You're a wonderful Queen. And wife. And mother. You always manage to get these things done. And I appreciate everything you do."

"I know you do..." Queen Annabel sighed. "Though if this works the way you're hoping it will – the way *we* are hoping it will," she corrected herself as Papa made a noise, and Thony could almost hear her rolled eyes, "then the poor boy will miss out on all the romance of finding his *own* princess."

"It will only be a betrothal," King Bill soothed. "He's not old enough to be married yet. I'll offer that the girl can come stsy here so they can get to know each other. And then you'll have a daughter-in-law presumptive to write out the invitations for the wedding."

"True." Queen Annabel sighed again. "I just wish..."

"I know," her husband agreed. "I wouldn't have wanted to miss out on coming across you weaving those nettle-shirts for your brothers, either."

"*They* weren't too happy about it," Mama said a little dryly. "And after all the trouble Papa went to in finding a witch who could cast the spell to turn them into swans."

Papa – *Thony's* papa, not Grandpa Dave – chuckled. "They just didn't think it would take quite so long. And Joe *is* ten years older than you and had just gotten married himself. Those nettles *did* give me lots of excuses to kiss your hands, though."

A low laugh from Mama. "I remember *that* quite well..."

They were... starting to sound more sugary than Thony really wanted to listen to. And he'd heard what he *needed* to hear, anyways. And it wasn't the confirmation that Papa and Mama's fairytale meeting had been contrived. *(Most of them were, after all. There was no particular shame in it.)*

They were going to throw the big party for his *fifteenth* birthday. Which was just two months away.

And Papa was going to find a way to secure a betrothal, even though Thony was underage. And even though everyone likely still remembered about Prissy's tail. And the story of Joanna and Priscilla and Roger running off together and then coming back with assorted sundry characters was still pretty fresh. Not to mention the lovely little scandal because Word had leaked out that Roger and Joanna's wedding had been *after-the-fact.*

This... was bad.

Really, really... *really* bad.

The only thing King Bill would be able to offer in exchange for one of the other kings to be willing to let a family member marry into the Devinthal's Bad Blood would be the promise that, if Thony died without male issue, Aldyrwald's three valleys would become part of the other king's demesne... or his son's, as the timing would probably have it. Which meant it would have to be one of the adjoining valley-kingdoms to even *begin* to make sense.

And not only did Thony *know* all the princesses in those kingdoms *(and think they were all jerks after the way they'd behaved at his sisters' parties)* but there would be a strong incentive for the offered bride to be well-past child-bearing years. Meaning at least double his age. Or possibly even older than *Mama*, which she likely hadn't thought about in her desire to have him marry a woman to serve as her social secretary.

Not to mention that since *none* of the valley-kingdoms was larger than three valleys right now *(Thony had heard that there was one far to the northwest that had four)*, this could seriously destabilize the region since it would potentially mean that one of their neighbors would be double the size of any of the other nations. Likely even just the *rumor* that such a betrothal was being considered could upset the rather delicate balance of power.

Of course, that meant that there was a much greater incentive for a king from a one- or two-valley kingdom to offer a sister – or even an aunt. And while the potential of creating violent conflict might be less if Thony ended up marrying – say, the fifty-something-year-old Princess Marian of the one-valley kingdom of Eidersparg – it still would end up turning Eidersparg into the largest country in the region.

Thony didn't want to believe that even the royal jerks in the surrounding countries would stoop to assassination... But given that they *were* such jerks, and with the ripe plum of Aldyrwald theirs if they could just get rid of its newly-crowned king... and once they started thinking like *that*, what difference would it make to kill off one young king that they might have to wait decades till he was crowned? Why not start *now*, with *Papa*, get Thony crowned, and then off him immediately?

In fact, why not promise a certain amount of independence to his soon-to-be-not-so-grieving widow and have her do the dark deed – or deeds – herself?

Thony's impression was that most royal princesses didn't want to have anything to do with ruling a country, but there were always some outliers. And while the youngest princess and *usually* the eldest princess in any lucky-numbered set *(three, seven, or twelve)* could pretty much guarantee finding a prince, that left a rather large number of middle-born girls whose best hope was to marry a lord within their father's kingdom. Or become a Princess-Aunt.

Not that the father or brother or nephew *(or grand-nephew, horror of horrors)* who was king would give the woman *much* independence. Women weren't meant to rule *(Amanita's stories of her mythical homeland notwithstanding)*. Any woman who tried – unless she was serving as a very temporary regent to an only slightly underage son – soon found herself inundated with princes and knights all eager to solve the problem by accepting her hand in marriage. Thony had heard rumors that most of the Ruling Queens ended up marrying the least objectionable fellow who showed up simply to get rid of the rest – it wasn't really possible to tell them all to get lost without insulting their fathers and brothers back home, and hosting large numbers of otherwise indolent royalty could become pricey rather fast.

Papa... couldn't *possibly* have thought this whole thing through.

Thony realized he was leaning on the sill of the open window of his room and that time was a-wasting. Mama would be expecting him to show up very shortly for dance-practice. He'd have to table this problem and wait until he could talk to Joanna about it. Or Roger. Or even Priscilla, though she'd never paid all that much attention to the politics between the valley-kingdoms.

There were two months before his birthday, after all. It wasn't *that* urgent.

And he could do some investigating in the meantime to see if maybe he was blowing this whole thing out of proportion.

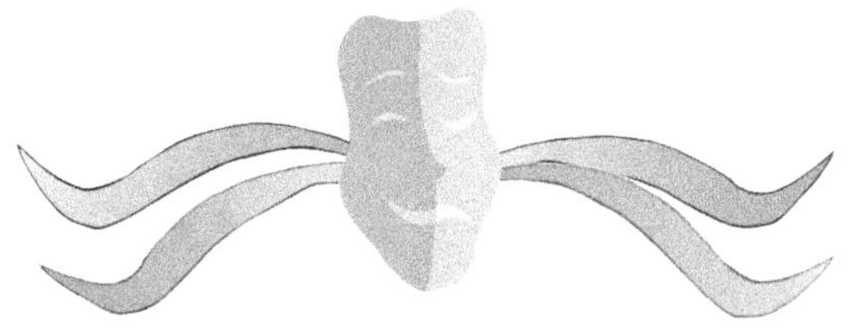

Chapter SEVEN

To Flee or Not to Flee – *That* is the Question

If Mama and Papa really wanted to keep the news of a too-early birthday bash under control, Thony mused as he was searching his father's desk late that night, they should have started by keeping the door to Mama's 'office' closed while they were discussing it. And then she should probably *leave* it locked if she was writing secret invitations in there.

King Bill at least locked his office, not that the lock hindered Thony at all.

Once he was in, it was a matter of sorting through the vast array of written notes. Some people thought out loud. King Bill thought in written form. However, if the organization of those notes on his desk indicated anything about the organization of his mind... well, Thony would say the kingdom was in trouble, but really, it wasn't a complex place to run, as he'd once pointed out to Joanna. And clearly it was from his father that Thony had inherited his, erm, *organizational approach*. Though that suggested King Bill's attitude about the mess in Thony's room had been hypocritical at best.

Luckily Papa also never seemed to notice when anything got moved around on his desk – which Thony totally would have if anyone had tried to mess with his stuff before, erm, they *totally messed with his stuff*. At least, he thought he would have. As far as he'd been able to tell, no one had ever tried anything other than gross 'adjustments' to his projects.

The young prince cleared a section of the desk and began sorting the various pages and notebooks and scraps of paper, based on content. There was a ridiculous number of comments on various meals. Some rather complimentary notes regarding Jeremy's parents. Reminders – buried under a slather (not even a stack) of other things – to get in touch with King Richie and Queen Janet to commiserate about their children. An entire series of sketched out arguments to make with Priscilla on Why it was Unwise to Marry Outside the Species.

And... yes. In an unexpectedly organized fashion, and near the top of one set of piles, was the Entire Plan. Thony was to be betrothed to whatever princess might be offered, with the 'bidding' to open on his fifteenth birthday. A set of neatly bulleted points listed out the concessions King Bill would be willing to consider in order to buy his son a bride – beginning with various trade options that were fairly standard in these cases, going through forced relocation of certain master craftsmen *(and had one of their neighbors really tried to kidnap Master Luke? Who needed a part-time artistic candlemaker that badly?)*, continued through the wholesale transfer of one of Aldyrwald's valleys... or possibly two.

And there it was. At the very end, scrawled in teeny, tiny writing in the margin, almost as if Papa didn't want to write it down, but had come to the realization that this might be the only choice: transfer of Aldyrwald and all its assets and territories to the princess' homeland upon Thony's death without male issue.

There were no other notations, so the young prince had no way of telling if the words had been added as a last-minute addendum because King Bill honestly hadn't thought about that option until he'd run out of paper... or if he'd added them reluctantly, hoping he could fill the sheet with enough other options that they wouldn't be necessary. And, if reluctantly... was that because it would mean the end of Aldyrwald as an independent valley-kingdom? The rule of the country was a trust, after all, handed down from a king to his son for his grandson and great-grandson as he had received it from his great-grandfather and grandfather via his own sire.

Or... had even the often flighty-seeming King Bill gone down the darker paths that this must surely lead to?

Thony carefully re-disorganized the papers on the desk and leaned back in Papa's chair, lacing his fingers behind his head and stretching out his legs. He had to think about this.

Surely it couldn't be *that* important to Papa that he marry a princess. Could it? If it was – why? Even if there was a local dearth of worthy miller's daughters, there were surely *some* in the neighboring kingdoms.

Well, the obvious answer was that his sisters' extremely unconventional lives had put Aldyrwald – put *the Devinthal family* – so far out of the social circles of the other royals that King Bill feared they could never come back. And if that was the case... how large a step was it to go from snubbing and disregarding to deciding that the Devinthals were *illegitimate* rulers, despite their long and storied past?

And *illegitimate* rulers were *meant* to be dethroned – and presented an opportunity for all those disenfranchised princes. Only one of them – probably a youngest son – would end up as the new king, of course, but the rest might well be able to oust the vassals of the *illegitimate* king and take over their lands. And with Aldyrwald consisting of *three* valleys, there was the potential for two – or even *three* – separate new kingdoms to be spawned from its ashes.

So, yes, any hint of illegitimacy must be eliminated.

But kings drew their legitimacy from the Gods, else kings would be overthrown by unhappy younger brothers all the time and on the flimsiest of pretexts. That didn't happen in the mountain region – Thony couldn't say about the rest of the world. *(It wasn't so much that he wasn't interested in the history and geography beyond the mountain region as that books and teachers on such were pretty thin on the ground.)*

Could the other royals be considering Priscilla's tail as evidence that the Gods had withdrawn their Blessings from Aldyrwald? Perhaps... After all, King Bill and Queen Annabel hadn't managed three *daughters*. They'd barely managed three *children*. *(Thony had some dark speculations as well about how the other royal families were able to generate such perfect numbers of children.)*

The prosperity of Aldyrwald would seem to speak against that sort of superstitious rot, but people could be stupid and stick to their preconceptions, even in the face of overwhelming evidence to the contrary. Look at how Great-Uncle Sir Eddie had defended 'his' decision for Thony to ride Silverfoot. Or how Mama and Papa did their best not to acknowledge Jeremy... or their daughters' changed status in general.

Thony rather doubted that Joanna and Roger and Priscilla would allow Aldyrwald to become a war-zone. In addition to their family being here, Joanna's Holy Mountain was here.

In fact, he rather doubted that his sister the Goddess of 'Love' *(he tried not to wince in memory of the rather detailed explanation Prissy had begun and from which he had fled)* nor his sister the Goddess of the Earth *(and all that implied in terms of fertility and fecundity)* would allow him to die without an Heir. No matter *how* old a wife the crowned kings foisted off on him.

But the young prince also knew that they were chary of using Their Divine Powers too broadly. He'd heard *(or overheard)* a lot of discussions about 'unintended consequences' and 'evolved systems' and the 'butterfly effect'. *(He'd had to ask about those last two. Roger had explained that 'evolved systems' were things like weather – a bit of air in a room didn't have weather, even if you had enough fans to blow it around quite a lot. But put <u>enough</u> air together and weather arose spontaneously. He'd gone on to try to explain that if you put enough weather together you got a 'climate', but Thony's brain had been too full right then for more information. Joanna trying to explain how a butterfly flapping its wings on the other side of the world could cause a storm in Aldyrwald had made him feel like his head was about to actually <u>explode</u>.)*

So exactly *what* or *how much* they might do to help out – and under what sorts of time-constraints – was, perhaps, questionable. Not to mention that putting all one's hopes in Gods and not doing what one could oneself was just asking for trouble *(even if those Gods were your sisters and brother-in-law)*.

So, *then* the question became 'what should Thony do *now*'?

That... wasn't at all clear.

Revealing what he'd discovered to his parents would not likely get him anywhere. Planning to marry him off or not, King Bill and Queen Annabel still seemed to see the baby in toddling pants he'd been twelve years ago when they looked at him. *(And clearly neither of them had followed out the likely consequence of this rash plan to Thony's princess-bride possibly being older than his mother. Because how could that possibly square with their view of him as barely more than an infant?)*

Sabotaging the party plans was eminently doable, but was unlikely to improve the Devinthals' situation in the views of their royal peers. The same went for sabotaging potential marriage negotiations.

He unlaced his fingers and ran a hand through the riot of his red curls. At least Thony and his sisters had one of the approved sets of coloration for three children in a family. If he'd been a girl, likely they'd have been nicknamed Snow-white, Merry-gold, and Rose-red. Or some such nonsense.

If Thony had been a *girl*, the family would also have met *one* set of royal expectations, and Priscilla would have been dismissed as an unimportant middle-born. Joanna's husband would have become Papa's Heir – so her hand would have been much sought-after *(though probably not by Roger, who wouldn't have had a chance against all the youngest sons)*. And Thony – in this imaginary incarnation as 'Rose-Red' would have had some fairytale arrangement to find an eldest-born prince, just as Mama had done.

If Thony had been a *girl*, in other words, there would have been no problem.

Even if Thony hadn't been born *at all*. There were enough fairytales about pairs of sisters as opposite as Joanna and Priscilla...

Hmmn.

No one outside Aldyrwald really believed that his sisters had become Goddesses.

Roger and Joanna were Properly Married – they'd had a big wedding celebration a few months back. All the neighboring royals had come in for that, dripping with curiosity. King Bill and King Richie had made it out as if they'd been *asked*, not just *informed*, and managed to imply that they'd been setting the children up for this from the very beginning because of their great friendship – that that was why Roger had served as a page and squire in Aldyrwald. Queen Annabel and Queen Janet had pasted smug and pleased looks on their faces. Priscilla had served as maid-of-honor, of course, and had possibly used a touch of Divine Power not to become excited and give their guests the show they were hoping for.

If Thony didn't exist... Aldyrwald's problems would be solved. From the perspective of politics, anyways.

Not that Roger and Joanna would be willing to rule after King Bill. They had made that Very Clear. They were content to pretend to be 'just folks', but it was a short-term pretense, not for the long run.

But perhaps... just for a year or so...

Nothing about the situation would have changed in a year *(or two... or even three)* but it would give Thony time to look for a better solution. To grow up a little bit. To – maybe – find a way to not be hitched to the petticoats of an old woman who was only waiting for a chance to off him.

To maybe... find his *own* princess. It was clear now that a miller's daughter wouldn't be sufficient to stave off the collapse of civility in the mountain region – or at least the destruction or dismemberment of Aldyrwald – no matter how worthy she might have proven herself. Even spinning straw into gold wouldn't do it.

He didn't want a wife *now*. But Thony was honest enough with himself – and about his future – to accept that a wife was something he would eventually have to *have*.

A princess-bride.

His future *Queen.*

The person he would spend the rest of his *(hopefully very long and peaceful, even if unutterably boring)* life with.

It would be okay if it was some mountain princess *(though, please, not one of the horrible neighbors)* and their parents contrived a fairytale meeting. The chance of it being someone he would actually fall in *love* with, like Joanna and Priscilla had done, was pretty small. Lightning might strike twice, but three times? The young prince was aware that most of the contrived fairytale meetings were between virtual strangers.

But Thony could *decide* to love her – whomever she turned out to be – like Mama and Papa had done. Or King Richie and Queen Janet. Or Uncle Louis and his mermaid.

A 'happily ever after' was what you *chose* for yourself.

Only, please let it not be to a woman older than his mother... and preferably someone who could also be a friend. Someone a little more like his sisters than that gaggle of gossiping geese in his mother's solarium or the heartless creatures in the neighboring kingdoms.

But in order to find that princess – or to give his parents time to find her – Thony needed to not be *here*. He couldn't be betrothed *in absentia*, after all. And if he wasn't here, then Roger and Joanna...

He *couldn't* ask his sisters' advice, Thony suddenly realized in surprise. Joanna – and Roger – wouldn't be pleased to be tied down to Aldyrwald while *he* gallivanted around the world.

And more than that.

Roger was God of Wind, and Joanna was Goddess of Earth. They would be able to find him and bring him back to Aldyrwald no matter where he went... on... *this*... world.

There was only one solution.

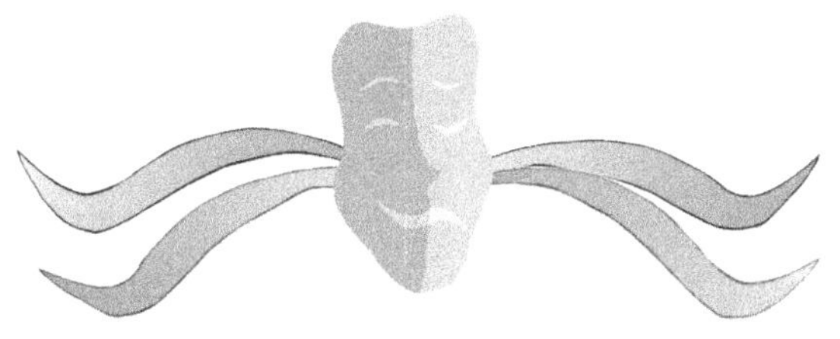

Chapter EIGHT

Deserted

THERE WASN'T A HUGE URGENCY. It wasn't like he had to set out today or tomorrow, though it would be better to be gone before Mama could send out the invitations and then have to send out retractions. Though at the speed Mama wrote – since she *couldn't* ask Joanna or Priscilla for help, she *wouldn't* ask Thony, and she apparently *daren't* ask her ladies-in-waiting – that gave him at least a week.

Since he couldn't consult with Joanna, Thony went for the next best option: his *new* best friends.

He headed down early the next day to capture Amanita and Wesley for an hour before his usual excursion with Silverfoot. Amanita was scrubbing algal growth from a trough and Wes was cleaning currycombs when the young prince arrived at the stables. Neither task was so delightful as to prevent them from following his lead with alacrity.

Tad was willing, as always, to release them for a bit. The consideration wasn't because of Thony's rank or any other favoritism for these two; so long as he knew who was where and all the work got done in the end, Tad never minded if his helpers took some time off. It was a marked difference from the Chief Cook.

Thony led them all out to the sacrificial lot, which the tricksy trio had dramatically renamed the 'Desert Pasture'. It was a dusty, fenced-in area with hard-pounded dirt where livestock were kept when brought in to the village for sale. It would often be packed so tightly when several shepherds or cowherds brought in their beasts all at once that the animals could barely mill around. They were never in there for long, but the numbers of them ensured that the ground was packed down too hard for plants, and hungry beasts snatched up what brave blades of grass or dandelions attempted a roothold there. It was the ground itself that had been sacrificed to this purpose, and Thony had noticed that Joanna avoided the place.

It hadn't been that easy to tell, given that she rarely had reason to come out this far from the castle, but he'd gone with her one day when someone had asked her down to the village to visit with a new mother and baby. She'd given the place a dark look and circled wide around it. And that had been *years* before she'd become Goddess of the Earth. Thony rather suspected She'd like the damaged soil even less now, but had to admit that it had been created for a reason and was ignoring it as thoroughly as Mama and Papa were Jeremy.

Which made it an ideal place to hatch a plan that *She* shouldn't hear about.

It was also a wonderfully still day – in other circumstances Thony would be just about *dying* for a breeze with the sun beating down on them – but since he was trying to plan without being caught by his brother-in-law, the Lord of the *Wind*...

"So, what's up?" Wes asked once they were all perched rather precariously on the top edge of the post-and-rail fence. "This isn't one of *my* favorite places. The dust makes my nose itch."

"I want your complete attention," Thony told the two of them. "And no distractions."

"An itchy nose is a distraction," Wes complained.

Thony rolled his eyes. "Bother your nose. This is *important*. And *serious*. I have a big problem. My parents are planning a huge birthday party for me."

"That doesn't sound like a *problem*, Thony," Wes replied, scratching at his nose. "That sounds like one heck of a good time."

"No," Amanita looked a bit more serious. "I've been listening around and the only time the royals in these valley-kingdoms do this sort of thing is when they're making it clear that their kid is available to be wed." She frowned. "But aren't you not old enough for another year?"

Thony nodded, pleased that she, at least, was actually listening. "They're doing this a full year early. I think – no, I *know*, I hunted around in Papa's office and got *proof* – that, after all the crazy with my sisters, they think I'm not likely to find a bride the normal way. So, Papa is planning to talk to the various kings at the party and... pretty much sell Aldyrwald to whichever one of them is willing to trade me a bride. The country will belong to that other king if I die without an Heir of my own."

Amanita made a face. "That means they'll be sticking you with some older woman that they can't get rid of any other way." She looked thoughtful. "She'd have a pretty good incentive to keep you alive and make sure you ended up with an Heir, though. Better to be queen of her own kingdom than the forgotten maiden-aunt in her brother's. Or nephew's. I've heard about what happens to these 'extra' princesses," she added darkly.

Thony waved a hand at that. "Most of them marry 'down' into the lesser nobility. It's no worse than the middle-born sons. *They're* all stuck earning their shields and then wandering from place to place, always knowing that they'll never find a permanent home. Actually," he said thoughtfully, "the girls probably have it better. But that's not the issue right *now,*" the young prince added hastily as Amanita opened her mouth and the look in her eye said she was taking umbrage at something he'd said. She was... very *adamant* about what she called "women's rights". "The problem right *now* is what can I do to keep this from happening?"

He didn't want to tell them his own idea. That would likely keep them from being as creative and send all the discussions down a particular path. Thony was hoping they – with their outsiders' viewpoint – might see an option he had missed.

Letting them weigh in had worked already. It hadn't occurred to *him* that the older princess he'd be saddled with would have any reason *not* to follow her father's or brother's *(or, please not her nephew's or grand-nephew's)* directives. He hadn't really gotten around to thinking about things from the woman's perspective. Though it seemed likely that any princess so offered would be chosen for her biddability and loyalty to her home kingdom...

"I don't know, Thony," Wes joked, "it might not be all bad. They say older women–"

The rest of what he might have said was lost as Amanita thwacked him a good one and Wes lost his balance and fell off the fence, raising a great pouf of dust. The girl had nearly unbalanced herself as well, and paused in glaring at the fallen youth to move herself down one rung so that she could hold on with her arms draped over the top, as well as tuck her ankles around the lowest rail.

"Well, definitely not *younger* women," Wes had stood up and was dusting himself off. "Avoid those, Thony. They're violent."

Thony rolled his eyes. "*I'm* not even old enough to be wed at *all*, Wes. There won't *be* anyone younger than me available. And the goal of the kingdom she's coming from would be to make sure I didn't have an Heir. And preferably died young, so they could take over Aldyrwald that much sooner. I had been thinking my 'bride' would have orders to poison me or something." He nodded at Amanita. "I hadn't realized she might have an incentive to keep me whole."

A small one anyways.

"Well, until you have an Heir," Amanita pointed out. "Then she's better off without you. She can serve as Queen-Regent and ditch this whole stupid male-dominated system. With – how long is it till someone can legally rule in their own name? Age twenty? With that long, she might even be able to train up the little dude to realize *women* are capable of doing great things."

Lovely. So even the 'good' scenario ended with him killed off early.

Thony eyed her cautiously. "Twenty-one, actually. Three times seven, so it's twice over a magickal number. Queen-Regents around here tend to get swamped with knights and princes vying for their hand – unless the Heir is close to being crowned."

"A woman so old *you* don't want to marry her isn't likely to have that 'problem'," Amanita pointed out.

She might be right, but she'd phrased it to make it sound like Thony was an incredible jerk. It wasn't as if he wanted to marry *anyone* right now, after all. Of *any* age.

Not to mention that with a kingdom as her dowry, there would be a lot of landless younger sons who'd marry a crone if they had to. Stepfather to the king-in-waiting... and so many terrible and permanent things could happen to a small boy...

"So, what do you want us to do?" Wes asked, choosing to lean on the fence this time, rather than perch. "Prank the party so it's a mess?"

Thony shook his head. "No, that just makes relations with the neighbors worse." He winced. "Trust me, I did that after they were all awful to Prissy at Joanna's sixteenth birthday party and it did *not* help anything."

"What did you do?" Amanita asked curiously.

The young prince winced. "It doesn't matter. Let's just leave it at saying that's why the Chief Cook doesn't want me anywhere near the kitchens."

She looked... impressed. "That was like ten years ago, wasn't it?"

"I told you, he doesn't do second-chances," Thony reminded her. "So, no, I don't want to prank the party. The *problem* is that the neighbors won't be willing to marry anyone into our family, and if I don't marry a real princess, Papa seems to be concerned that will *prove* that the Devinthals no longer have the Divine Right of Kings... which will make it open season on overthrowing us."

Wes' eyes crossed. "If *you guys* don't have the right to rule, then who possibly could?"

The appearance of the mountain had sort of convinced most of the Local Populace that Joanna was a Goddess. And enough of them had seen Priscilla running around in centaur-form with Jeremy that they were willing to believe in Her as well. *(Which meant that Prissy's 'secret' was probably very term limited and she should probably tell Mama and Papa before they found out from someone else it was always more of a mess when that happened. Thony had experience in these things and he knew.)* He wasn't sure if anyone realized Roger was also a God... but it was likely just a matter of time.

Thony sighed. "You know that outside of Aldyrwald no one really gets that, right?"

"Yeah..." Wes gave him a sideways look. "Actually, they're still kind of iffy about it in the other Aldyrwald valleys, from what I hear."

"That'll work itself out in the next few hundred years, Joanna says," Thony told them. He didn't add that Jo had started tearing up when she said it. It had been what convinced him that he was just as glad that he, also, hadn't been Chosen to become a God, no matter how much fun it sounded like to have all that Power. Living forever, it had been brought home to him rather abruptly, meant saying goodbye to the people you loved over and over and over again. Someday he'd be old and passing on his throne *(well, if he could derail Papa's plans)* to his own son and lying on his deathbed... and Joanna and Priscilla would still be young.

Amanita nodded wisely. "Well, that's likely true. People take time to get used to changes." She scowled a bit. "And some of them just get *old* and *bitter* and are *miserable to the rest of us* over how the things *they* wanted didn't *turn out.*"

It was the look she wore when she was talking about her father's mother. Wes had managed to get out of her that she had four aunts on that side of the family and *they* were all great people. And a number of cousins from those aunts. He'd also teased out that her mother's name was Ytheril and her father's was Naeel – which were as foreign as her own name and told the boys absolutely nothing useful. But it was a little more detail on her past.

"Hmmn." Thony looked at the position of the sun. "I need to get going soon if I'm to meet Roger – or Jeremy. Do you guys have any ideas for me?"

Wes frowned.

Amanita laughed. "You could run away from home. They can't marry you off if you're not here."

Wes snorted as Thony held his breath. "He wouldn't do that, 'Nita. The Heir to the Throne can't just *run off.*"

She looked out over the 'Desert Pasture' and dangled one foot off the fence to kick up some dust. "Well, we've got two months to come up with something, right? It's not *urgent* or anything."

Thony wanted to say he thought he needed a plan *rather sooner* than that. But he wasn't sure how to say it without sounding all bossy and princely. Or without implying that he already had *a* possible plan. Especially after what Wes had just said about how he wouldn't run off.

It was frustrating, and he felt like they weren't really taking his concern all that seriously, for all that they seemed to understand the problem.

"I should get back to work, too," Amanita sighed.

"Yeah, those currycombs are waiting for me," Wes added.

"With their teeth out, no doubt," Thony joked, hoping he'd sound like his normal self, rather than showing his frustration.

They all laughed and went back to the barns.

It was just Jeremy again today, which was a relief to Thony. He really had to think through his options before facing Roger – or Joanna – again.

The trouble was, his *options* category didn't seem to have anything in it besides the one, Really Bad Idea.

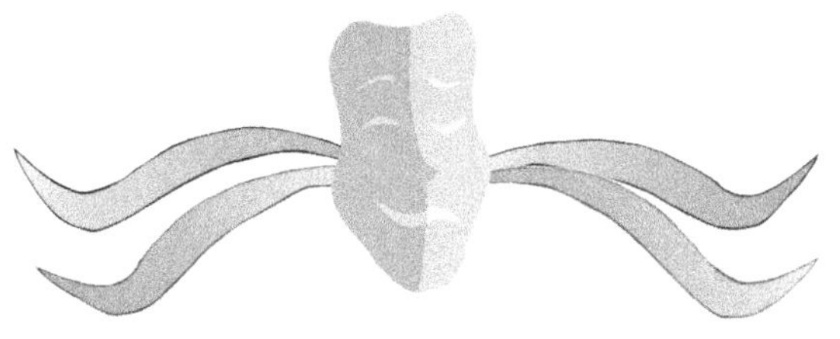

Chapter NINE

Just Desserts

THE REST OF THE WEEK went pretty much as normal.

Rides and secret lessons with Jeremy – Roger never showed, and Joanna was missing, too.

Riding lessons with Great-Uncle Sir Eddie.

Dancing lessons in Mama's solarium.

Protocol lessons with Master Eswith.

Dinner with the Court.

Every night, Thony checked the progress of the invitations in Mama's office. And for new information in Papa's.

He could easily have slowed down the process by damaging some of the invitations – Mama was careless with her cups of tea, and her ink, and was doing enough of that already that a bit more wouldn't really be noticed – but that wouldn't really do anything other than make the lives of the staff harder. The Chief Cook and the castle's Chatelaine wouldn't be informed until the invitations were sent out, he had determined. Giving them less time to prepare was cruel – unless he could come up with something that would derail the whole event entirely.

He found himself being evasive with Wes and Amanita after he tried to bring up the subject a couple other times and they brushed off his concerns in the same, absent-minded way Silverfoot flicked flies with his tail. Amanita wanted to focus on getting David back and felt they had plenty of time to get to Thony's problem after that.

Her current favorite plan was to fill David's shoes with slugs while he slept.

Wes preferred getting David in trouble with the Head Pastry Chef – who was only second to the Chief Cook and could *certainly* not be replaced right before a major party was planned. A wry nod to Thony acknowledged the reason for that party. He also pointed out that getting into David's room and then making sure the slugs *stayed* in his shoes was a problem, slugs not being notable for staying where you put them.

Thony waved off the first concern – he could pick any lock in the castle, he assured them. However, he didn't see how really gross feet would teach David the lesson they wanted. Though it *would* be a worthy revenge.

"The next girl he tries that on won't likely have your skills," he pointed out to Amanita. "Or your moxy. And she probably won't report him to anyone. He's not a particularly *bad* person right now – just a spoiled one. But if he starts to get away with things like this, he's going to go rotten pretty fast."

"*I'd* say he's rotten already," she grouched. "And totally deserves slugs in his shoes."

"I can't argue with that," Wes noted, but he looked a little uncomfortable.

Thony gave his tall friend a slight smile, but focused on Amanita. "Actually, I think he's probably just shy. He liked you and he didn't know how to tell you. He's one of those people who's better with *doing* stuff than talking about it. And – when you're not mad at someone – you're a pretty friendly person. He may have been watching and seen that you were nice to him and gotten the Wrong Idea."

She narrowed her eyes. "So, you're saying this is *my* fault?"

"Not at all!" Thony shook his head vehemently and waved his hands in front of him in a gesture of denial. "He should have had the manners to say something, even if it was hard. And then to *listen* when you weren't interested. I'm just saying that he needs a lesson, but maybe not punishment."

"I've heard he yelled at his dad about firing you," Wes volunteered, still looking awkward and avoiding her eyes.

Amanita folded her arms. "So, I'm supposed to think he's a great guy now?"

The young prince sighed. "No. I'm just saying it's not a crime to like you. As a *girl*, not just as a friend. Or it shouldn't be, anyways. You're pretty, you're friendly, you're smart. It's going to happen eventually. Again. And hopefully the guy is more upfront about things and actually *says* something to you instead of trying to just *show* you."

And hopefully some of that got through to *Wes* before *he* did something that messed up their friendship.

Amanita looked a little horrified. "You're not saying that *you–*"

Thony traded her horrified look for horrified look. "No. Of course not. Don't be ridiculous. But most people get married someday. And if you're lucky, like my sisters, it's to somebody whom you actually *like.*"

It was an issue he was rather sensitive about right now for himself after all.

He did *not* dare look at Wes himself. Thony had a great deal of practice at keeping his inner thoughts from showing on his face – even aside from not letting on about his pranks, there was a lot of benefit to such control at Court – but the large stableboy wasn't nearly so practiced at it.

The girl's expression became sympathetic. "Thony, you're still worried about that party, aren't you. I told you; we'll work on that after we deal with David."

He rolled his eyes. "Fine. Then pick a plan. But it should be something to teach the guy that he needs to use his words, not just take what he wants. Slugs won't help with that." Thony nodded at Wes. "Wes' idea has some potential. If we can figure out how to make it work." His eyes went far away. "David's super-proud of his stew-making skills, right? And I have to admit, his stuff is really good. But he wants to follow his father as Chief Cook and that means he needs to learn about *all* the things that are made in the kitchen. I think I can get Mama – or the Chatelaine – to suggest that David should do a turn as an apprentice pastry chef."

Amanita started to look riled – after all, that had been the position that she'd just lost when he met her. But Wes was looking interested. He nodded vigorously.

"That was always the weakness in my plan. From what I've heard, there's currently no reason for David and the Head Pastry Chef to have much to do with each other. Didn't one of you say that even the prep work happens in two different areas?"

"That would have been me." Amanita sounded sour, but she looked like she was getting interested in spite of herself. "Different tools, different tables, different ovens. We – *they* –

have their own cold room and pantry as well. The shared stuff is the sinks, and mostly that's handing tools to the dishwashers to be cleaned. And occasionally if the dessert requires something more commonly used for the savory dishes." Her eyes went wide, then her face settled into a smirk. "Then *Mr. Make-the-Stew* and *Mr. Grabby-Hands* have to deal with *each other*. Oh, this will *not* be pretty."

She rubbed her hands in glee.

Thony reflected that it was interesting that she hadn't decided to call *David* 'Mr. Grabby-Hands', all things considered. Apparently, it was either already taken, or she was still more upset over Paul taking her pastry tools than with David trying to kiss her. Interesting.

Not to mention that – even if he *had* been thinking about Amanita the way she hadn't entirely suggested – that look of unholy delight in the coming mayhem would have convinced him otherwise. She was everything he could want as a partner in pranking... but the queen who would rule beside him should be more concerned with the possible fallout. This girl would be an unmitigated disaster if she sat on a throne. "Women's rights" and their abilities to rule notwithstanding.

Well. At least *that* was never going to happen.

"They've known each other at least as long as *I've* known them," the young prince warned her. "I don't think they particularly *like* each other, but they may have figured out how to work together a long time ago. *Years* in the kitchen, after all."

Amanita shook her head, still looking gleeful. "I don't think so. They always seemed to stay on opposite sides of the kitchen. And I think the Chief Cook and Head Pastry Chef know it. But if the word comes down from your mother that 'David is to be trained in all aspects of running the castle kitchens'..."

The small girl put on an affected air that Thony couldn't help comparing to his mother's tone when passing on instructions to the servants. The Chatelaine or her lady's-maid, usually, since she couldn't be expected to speak to anyone below their rank. Except possibly for a more detailed consultation with the Chief Cook or Head Pastry Chef about what she wanted prepared, and *that* happened once in a blue moon.

"If this is done right, they'll both learn some valuable lessons – and we won't have to do a thing but sit back and watch the fireworks," Wes approved.

While he was an inveterate prankster in the stables – where everyone seemed to do a certain amount of it – he was much more chary of anything that happened outside his area of comfort and tended to advocate a 'less is more' approach. The castle was *definitely* outside his comfort zone.

Amanita, however, was definitely a '*more* is *more*' type.

"Nonsense," she said haughtily. "With a little effort we can get them *both* back."

Wes looked nervous.

Thony clapped him on the back. "First things first. I don't know how long it's going to take to get Mama on board with interfering in the kitchens."

First, he'd have to draw her attention to the excellent stews they'd been eating for the last year, and *then* reveal that they were being prepared by the Chief Cook's son. And *then* work her around to the thought that the young man should be groomed to replace his father someday... and *only then* float the idea of an internship in the desserts department.

He grinned at Amanita. "Don't worry. I'm sure they'll both get their just desserts."

She rolled her eyes and Thony had to head back up to the castle for his dancing lesson.

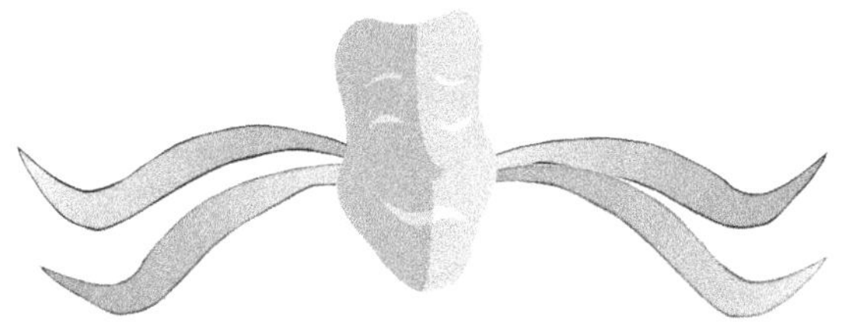

Chapter TEN

Ok, This is Getting *Serious*

MOVING *THAT* PROJECT ALONG WAS easier than coming up with a new plan for himself.

Mama wasn't intrinsically *opposed* to any of his comments, and seemed to take them well. Like his rats, it was relatively easy to get her to do things she was more or less inclined to do on her own anyways... even if it involved modifying the behavior a bit to meet Thony's preferences.

In fact, she seemed to be pleased that he was taking an interest in the running of the castle. *(To which he wanted very much to reply that he'd always taken an interest in the running of the castle; she'd just never appreciated his extremely numerous and creative demonstrations of that in the past.)*

And... somehow that led to the *next* conversation he overheard between her and Papa.

In her office again, and about the same time of day. Thony estimated that he had about two more days before the invitations were ready to be posted.

The potted plant had just been watered this time, however, and apparently its fronds had also been misted with water for some mysterious reason known only to whomever was in charge of the castle's indoor plants. Thony was grateful he was wearing riding clothes that were allowed to get wet and grungy and hadn't yet changed over to an afternoon suit for dancing class, since those fabrics would be much less forgiving.

"– turning into quite the responsible young man," Mama was saying approvingly. "Quite mature for his age."

"Good," King Bill said. "It's time he started acting like a young man instead of a boy. Especially since I've had a response. Just today."

What?!?

Queen Annabel made some fluttery noises. "When you said you wanted the invitations to go out as I finished them, I thought you said you'd save discussing that with anyone until the party itself."

King Bill sighed. "I know. But there's really only a handful of our neighbors with appropriate girls. And there are some we'd definitely prefer to the others. Some *he'd* definitely prefer, but you as well, my dear. I don't imagine you want a daughter-in-law old enough to be *your* mother."

Now *that* thought was enough to make Thony blanch and feel a bit ill. Even his *own* imagination hadn't carried him *that* far.

"Certainly not," Queen Annabel huffed. "But I'd like a look at the girls."

"You've seen them all before, sweetheart," her husband reminded her. "At Jo and Roger's wedding, most recently."

"I wasn't considering them as possible daughters-in-law then!"

"No... but beggars can't be choosers," King Bill said a little heavily. "We have to make this happen. And by offering a man the assurance that a middle-born daughter of his will actually be a *queen...*"

Mama made a sound like she was deflating. "I suppose. We can still arrange for a proper fairytale meeting, though... no?" Her voice sounded... strange.

Thony imagined Papa shaking his head sadly. "No, sweetheart. We'll be announcing the betrothal at the party. To make it clear that everything is all locked away and settled. And with the wedding to follow as soon as is decent."

"Oh..." Mama sounded disappointed. "I... suppose there's no point anyways. For a *middle-born princess.* I may have met them, Bill, but I never paid any attention to *those* girls."

Mama sounded disappointed?

Thony was *horrified.*

He stumbled out from behind the plant, making enough of a clatter that King Bill called out to ask who was out there.

The young prince didn't answer. He went to his rooms and sank down in a squat in one corner, elbows on knees, head in hands, backside braced against the connected walls.

This... was a *disaster.*

How had he not found Papa's ranked choices of nearby princesses? It must be somewhere in that pile. Papa never, *ever* thought anything he didn't immediately write down. He actually carried a pocket full of paper and a stub of a pencil everywhere to note things down throughout the day and emptied his pockets on his desk before bed each night.

Of course, Thony had never actually made it to the *bottom* of any of those piles. Once he'd found what he thought he needed, he'd quit looking.

Papa would be sending a response *tonight*, it sounded like. Tomorrow at the latest. And it sounded like the answer would be 'yes'. What concessions had Papa already offered? Did Thony even dare hope that he'd only opened negotiations and not given away the kingdom already?

He ran through the names of the princesses – the *middle-born* princesses – in all the adjoining countries. Though if that was the tack Papa was taking – promising a queenship to a girl who'd likely never otherwise even be wedded – perhaps he hadn't given away the kingdom after all. That might extend the options to the girls *two* kingdoms out.

But... a middle-born princess... and there *were* still all those Princess-Aunts... including the ones as old as his *grandmothers*, horror of horrors.

At least... at least Papa seemed to be trying to spare him *that* fate.

Although he didn't seem to have ruled it out.

Surely whichever princess was highest on Papa's list – the one for whom he'd had that *response* – surely, *she'd* be younger. Still older than Thony, of course, but not... not *old*.

It was early in the day, but if he could get into Papa's office and look at that letter...

But to have a chance at that – at *anything* – he had to make it look like nothing was wrong. That, at least, was something the young prince had plenty of experience at. One had to maintain a straight face – or at least a context-appropriate one – when waiting for a prank to culminate, after all.

He ran through the steps in his head. Shower, change, dancing lesson. Then he should have a few hours before dinner.

The letter would probably be on top of everything else. Possibly, for something this important, Papa would even manage to *keep* it on top of everything else. Thony would only need a few minutes...

The hours dragged. His dancing was apparently better than ever, however. Distracted as he was, Thony followed directions mechanically, even to looking at his partner's face and taking a more sure grip on her waist.

Finally, he was freed, and he headed off to lurk in the area near Papa's office.

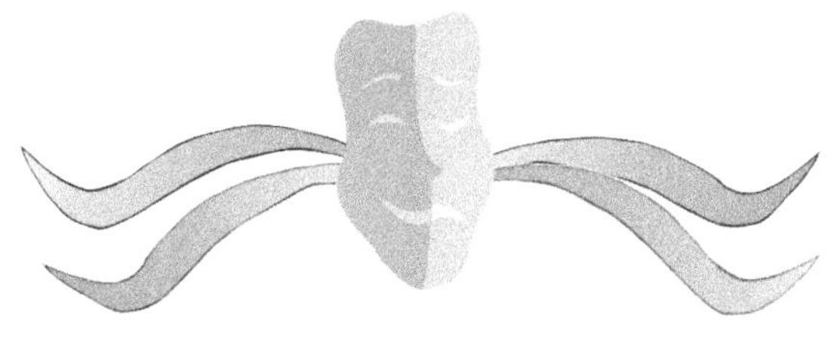

Chapter ELEVEN

"Bad Blood"... *Sucks*

NATURALLY, THIS WOULD BE THE *one day ever* that King Bill decided to spend the afternoon in his office. Was he possibly composing an answer already? Had more *responses* come in? *(Surely Papa hadn't made the same offer to multiple kings at once. Though a bidding war over the opportunity to seat a middle-born daughter on the throne of Aldyrwald might reduce the concessions that would have to be made to overcome the perception of Bad Blood.)*

Thony nearly jumped out of his skin more than once, scaring whatever servant had startled him as well. Fortunately, the staff was used to seeing him lurking in odd places and took it in good part after their initial surprise. Likely the word was being passed around that the Crown Prince was plotting something nefarious and/or amusing in this part of the castle.

At last *(at last)* Papa departed, carefully locking the door as he headed out for his afternoon constitutional. A creature of habit, the king was. Well, except for *staying* in his *office* for *half the afternoon* today.

Thony checked carefully to be sure there was no one around, then sauntered out in the open to fiddle with the knob, a slight frown on his face as if he had every right to be entering and was somewhat puzzled to find the room locked. Normally, he wouldn't have considered doing this until after everyone else was in bed, but this was an *emergency*. And acting like everything was normal would get him farther than sneaking around and acting devious.

The lock yielded to his skills as quickly as ever, and he slipped in and shut the door behind himself quickly.

Yes, there was an envelope in the center of the desk, facing the chair, its seal broken. Crisp sheets of – oh my gosh, *actual parchment* – were contained in the packet that was itself made of folded *vellum* and not mere paper.

Thony's eyes scanned quickly, pulling out particular details. The name of the king – written neatly below the royal scrawl and seal of the other country. The name of the other country. No mention of acceptance of specific terms that King Bill might have proposed, just a general agreement that the details could be negotiated when they arrived here in person.

And not a mention of the name of the princess to be his bride. Merely a note that the king had '*several* possible maidens who might fit the need'. Maidens who were 'eligible, demure, and skilled in all the maidenly arts'. If that wasn't the *squirreliest* way of insinuating that a girl more appropriate to betroth to a fifteen-year-old boy might be offered in return for more concessions... clearly King Howard of Liepbaum was well aware that he had the upper hand.

Thony's panicking mind couldn't recall the names and ages of all the Liepbaum princesses.

Was there a copy of King Bill's original letter? Thony needed to see what might already have been offered – or given away.

Besides *himself*, that was.

He started hunting and missed the sound of a hand on the doorknob.

Not the sound of the door opening, though there wasn't time to hide anyways. Not that it would have helped if he'd heard the knob, since Papa's desk was basically just a table without a concealed space beneath it and there was absolutely nowhere else that could even be remotely envisioned as a hiding place.

"Thony?" To his credit, King Bill's voice was neither surprised nor disappointed. "I take it you're aware of what is being planned. As you usually are."

If there was a touch of wryness in that assessment, Thony didn't notice it. He couldn't do anything besides nod.

His father's eyes were kind. And sad.

"I suppose I should have just given you a key to this office years ago and saved us all the pretense." The king walked around the desk and seated himself. "Do you want to sit down and talk about it?"

"No, sir." Thony was going to face this standing.

King Bill hesitated, then nodded. "Very well. You're aware of how we've been treated by the neighbors. Well, except for Richie, of course. What you probably *don't* realize is how different things were before Priscilla was born." He looked down at his hands, which had picked up a slender silver pen and were turning and twisting it. "Before *that*, actually. When your mother took so long to carry a second child to term... we'd become objects of scandal already. There didn't seem to be any reason, after all. And then it became pity after we lost so many babes... so many *children*. And then, when it seemed Joanna would be our only one, the neighbors became..."

"*Greedy,*" Thony volunteered as his father's words faltered. He wasn't sure how to take this newly serious version of his father – Thony had never before thought of all those miscarriages his mother had had as brothers and sisters that had died. But he *knew* what the neighbors were like.

King Bill looked up and met his son's eyes with a deep, old sadness. "No, Thony. Not *greedy*. Ambitious, maybe. Everyone has a youngest son who needs to find a princess who is her father's only Heir. You know how far my brother Louis had to go to find his. He's managed one visit back in all these years – to say goodbye to our father before he died. He says in his letters he's going to try to come see Mama before *she* passes. And bring up the children, so she can see them at least the once. But he's been saying *that* for five *years*. It's a mortal long distance to his kingdom on the sea."

Thony made a noncommittal sound. The idea of *Jo* being the object of a bidding war was hardly more attractive to him than the one about to be perpetrated over himself. Except that his sister's prospects wouldn't have included Aldyrwald being torn to shreds and a regional war being started that involved half the mountain kingdoms.

...no, *Jo's* 'prospects' would just have ended any chance of her actually marrying *her* true love...

Papa gave him a tired look. "Not to mention the five brothers between us, stuck serving as wandering knights-errant for all their days. We... produce too many royal children, here in the mountains. And we put too many expectations on them."

"Your brothers *could* marry peasant girls and have the hearth and home they talk about every time they visit," Thony said recalcitrantly, though this was getting pretty far off the topic he *wanted* answers for. The topic he *needed* answers for. "Or noblemen's daughters. Or middle-born princesses if they insist on such. They could even bring them here to live with us. You've told each of them that they're welcome to stay. And to bring home a bride. I've heard you."

King Bill nodded. "So they could. But a man wants to... be king of his own castle. However small it might be. So, I can see why they don't want to come back here. And unless they find an heiress *somewhere* – or settle for a peasant girl and build her a cottage and give up their skills and lineage to move rocks or hew timber all the rest of their lives – they'll always feel like they're living off my charity. Or yours, someday, as Uncle Eddie does, and resents every minute he's here."

Thony frowned. "But you'd give them useful things to do. Things you're paying *other* people to do *now*. You'd pay *them*, I'd imagine..."

His father was shaking his head. "It would hurt their pride if I even offered, Thony. I hinted at it and Ronnie didn't so much as send a letter for four years. Milt told me that it's what middle-born sons *do* – they earn their pay from other kings and keep an eye out for heiresses, however humble. The goal being to win the heart of the latter or save up the former so that when they come home at last, they can afford their own small house instead of merely a room in the castle. A small house and perhaps a widow to wed who'll keep their house and make their food and warm their –"

"I get it," Thony interrupted quickly, feeling his cheeks warm to match his hair.

His father gave him a small smile. "And your mother was saying today that you're all grown up. Not quite yet, it appears."

"What does any of this have to do with *me?*" Thony demanded, trying to ignore all of that. "Why do you have to put *me* up as a prize on the auction block – and a whole *year* before any of the *other* royal children have to deal with any of this? I'm not even *fifteen*, Papa," he added pleadingly, and trying not to tear up with frustration. "You were *twenty* when you and Mama got married, weren't you? Isn't it just the *girls* that have to wed early or not at all?"

"Well, except for our Jo, it appears," Papa snorted, but there was a pleased look under it for a moment. The pleased look went away as he focused on Thony again. "Plenty of royal children are betrothed as soon as they're born and the parents know if they're boys or girls."

Thony folded his arms. "Not any of *us*. Not *you*. Nor *Mama.*"

King Bill winced. "Your Mama was the youngest of seven daughters – crown princes were falling all over themselves to marry her. And Priscilla, well..." He winced again. "*I* was an eldest son – and Jo is an eldest daughter. As large as Aldyrwald is, we didn't need to make a treaty using her – or me – as coin."

"*I'm* an eldest son," Thony pointed out. "I'm an *only* son." He paused, then added, "It's because of the Bad Blood, isn't it. Same as for the girls."

His father hesitated, then nodded. "It's nonsense, of course–"

"And our neighbors are all idiots and *jerks,*" Thony commented bitterly. "Except for Roger's family."

One side of King Bill's mouth twitched up in something that... *wasn't* a smile. "Ah, yes, our *dear* friends of Schwannsberg. Not that Richie and Janet would ever have agreed to let Roger offer for Jo. Nor would they be willing to let *you* offer for Sophia. I asked them first," he admitted.

Sophia was Roger's middle-born sister. She was nearly twenty, Laura the eldest having been 'rescued' some years ago by a prince-and-Heir from a couple kingdoms farther north, and Tessa the youngest having been 'rescued' by the crown prince from the kingdom just past Richie's own a few months ago. Tess was sixteen.

Tess had also stood with the others and laughed at Priscilla just under a year ago.

Sophia... hadn't, but she hadn't exactly stood up and said anything either. At least not while Thony had been in the room. Whether that was from empathy or manners... or the timidity that so many middle-born princesses began to exhibit as their marital prospects waned... he had no idea.

He *might* have been able to forgive *Sophia* for not standing up for Prissy. Since she *hadn't* laughed.

But *King Richie*, Papa's best friend and Roger's father, had said he wouldn't accept an offer from Thony for his middle-born daughter. The daughter who was otherwise likely doomed to become a Princess-Aunt and look after her brother Raymond's children... and grandchildren...

Thony looked down. Sophia was older than Prissy and had always been somewhat quiet and withdrawn. He'd known her all his life as the two families had visited back and forth, but he'd never known her *well*. But she *was* Roger's sister. She... would have been... a better option than most of the others.

His father sighed. "I'm sorry, Thony. I... was hoping that this would all blow over. After Roger and Joanna wed, it seemed *possible*. But Richie..." He looked down at the pen now gripped in white-knuckled hands. "He's been my best friend since we were *boys*, Thony. Like our fathers before us. And he told me flat out that the only reason his *middle-born* son had married my oldest daughter was because they'd done it when they were gone and he couldn't forbid it. That Roger had told him to go ahead and *disown* him if he chose, and he'd have *done* so if not for Janet and Raymond begging him not to. That he'd have to be *dead* before he saw another one of his children marry another one of mine."

Thony dropped his stiff stance and came around the desk to kneel at his father's side and put his arms around him. "I'm sorry, Papa. I didn't know. You... you seemed fine. When you were with him. Talking, joking like normal."

King Bill pried a hand off the tortured pen and touched Thony's head. "That's what you were supposed to see, son. They're still our neighbors. And they're Roger's family. But... friends? Not... not so much anymore." He paused. "Though Richie did say that it wasn't *personal*. He just didn't want his family – his *kingdom* – linked more closely to ours."

The bitterness in the king's tone was... worn out. As if he couldn't put any energy even into anger over this anymore.

Not *personal*? How could it be anything *else*?

Thony let out a sigh and laid his head on his father's lap. "And... I can't wait for a worthy miller's daughter," he said resignedly. "I... figured that out. It has to be a princess, and her hand given willingly by her father. Or else we risk it being put about that we've lost the Divine Right of Kings."

Papa sighed as well. "You three have always been too clever for your own good."

"It's *my* fault," Thony added with his own bit of bitterness. "If I hadn't been born, *Jo* would be your heiress. And *she's* married. You wouldn't have *any* of these problems."

King Bill took Thony's shoulders in his and pulled him upright to look him in the eye. "Don't you *ever* think that, Anthony. *Easier* isn't always *better*. Your Mama and I went through... an awful lot to have you. *And* Priscilla. We wouldn't choose to have done anything else no matter how it's all turned out." He leaned back again, loosening his grip on Thony's shoulders and put on his best try at a humorous expression. "And this was the only way Joanna could have ended up with Roger, true love or not. Although I could wish that Prissy would have found a *human* to fall in love with – be he ever so humble. Caspar isn't a bad sort... so I suppose as long as his son treats her properly..."

He still looked a little uncertain. Worried.

"Prissy... turns herself into a centaur girl when she's out there with him," Thony knew he was breaking his word, but...

Papa's expression lightened. "Ah. I'd suspected something like that might be the case. That's... good. Better."

No need to mention that Jeremy had told Thony that her tail didn't transform into a proper horse-tail, so she didn't fit in with his herd all that much better than with humans. The centaur herd at least accepted Her as the Goddess She was and honored Her. Some of Jeremy's troubles with the fillies actually came *because* he was Priscilla's Chosen Mate.

"So... back to you," Papa said and Thony stiffened slightly. The king noticed and gave a little grim nod. "You've seen the response from King Howard."

" '*Several maidens*'," Thony quoted listlessly. "The only way he could make up that count is if he's including his own middle-born sister and aunt."

King Bill nodded. "I know, son. That's... a bargaining ploy. Howard is testing to see what I'm willing to offer him."

"A queenship for his middle-born daughter should be enough, *I'd* think," Thony said a little bitterly. Princess Stella was twenty-two. Her aunt was in her forties. Her *great*-aunt...

"Hmmn," Papa rubbed his bearded chin. "It's... *going* to be a princess who's older than you, Thony. I'll try to see it's not someone old enough to be your, um, mother. But one of the few pieces of bargaining power we have here is the ability to lock a betrothal into place before you'd otherwise be eligible."

Thony looked away. He wouldn't mention that he'd overheard Papa saying that they wouldn't wait the actual wedding any longer than was 'decent'... he *had* to assume that meant his sixteenth birthday. He *had* to because anything else was just... "I saw your list of *bargaining points*. That wasn't even on it. Nor was asking for the hands of middle-born princesses."

"Ah," King Bill said again. But he didn't add anything to it.

"Papa, we can't *give away* Aldyrwald."

"Do we have a choice, Thony?" King Bill asked sadly. "If you don't find a princess, the word will go out that we are no longer a true line of kings and Aldyrwald will be torn apart. If you marry a princess – an... *elder* princess... and die without an Heir of your own... at least the country will go over to someone else all in one piece. And peacefully."

Thony shook his head. "But that will upset the balance of power, Papa. Aldyrwald will be torn apart after that – or before, if the others suspect such a deal."

His father's chin dropped. "It's the best I can do, son. I... don't have any other ideas."

Thony looked into his father's eyes, his expression intent.

"I do. But... we can't tell Mama."

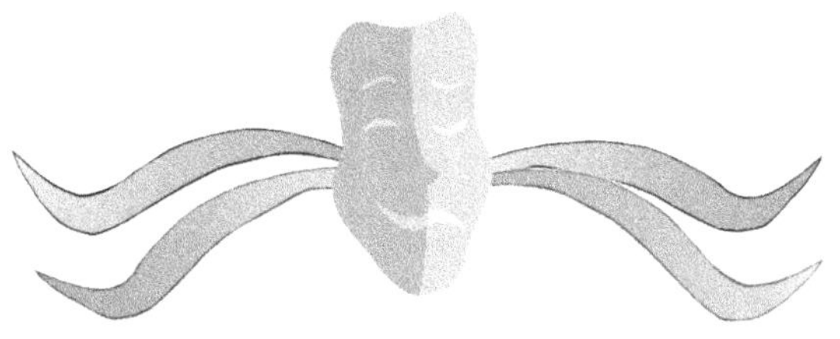

Chapter TWELVE

Immaturity Has Its Uses

DINNER THAT NIGHT WAS... CONTENTIOUS.

King Bill engaged Priscilla over the soup course over the issue of 'when was she going to listen to her parents and find a proper *human* prince'. Queen Annabel managed to stay out of it until halfway through the entrée. Her intervention – presumably *intended* to serve as a peacemaker, but she came down on her husband's side – only made things worse.

They'd all spent the last six months going over every possible argument and trying every possible *combination* of arguments to convince each other and had long since run out of new things to say. The only option left that any of the three of them could think of seemed to be to try to say the same things *louder* as if that would make the arguments themselves more acceptable.

It had become... a rather stunning departure for the Devinthals. King Bill was considered rather dreamy and flighty, Queen Annabel gentle and slightly ditzy, Princess Joanna quiet and wise, and Princess Priscilla sweet and a bit frivolous. If anyone was going to go off screaming it would have been most likely to be Thony – and he was good-natured, so the screaming would probably be out of excitement. *(Though most everyone tended to remember that he was often the source of that excitement...)*

Everyone but the family themselves fled before dessert was served. The ladies-in-waiting and senior squires and the handful of hired knights made phony excuses in desperation and disappeared the way Thony's rats had fled when Queen Annabel opened his door.

Tonight, that left the King, the Queen, Priscilla, Great-Uncle Sir Eddie and Thony – Joanna and Roger were off doing God-Things, as they had been all this week, and Grandma Lizzy ate in her rooms these days. Great-Uncle Sir Eddie looked like *he* would rather flee, but couldn't quite reconcile doing that with his self-image as a brave knight and the wise elder statesman of the family.

Thony had hunkered down a bit and waited for his moment.

That came when Mama and Papa and Priscilla had gotten to the point where they were *almost* yelling, but not quite. They would still be able to hear him, but be too bound up in their own internal conflicts that they weren't likely to come up with a rebuttal in the time he would allow them. Mama always let Papa go first, anyways, and tonight Papa was doing all this to create the diversion Thony had asked him to.

Glad that Joanna *(who could always see right through him)* and Roger *(who was nearly as adept at it)* were not there, Thony stood up suddenly and yelled, "Will you just stop it, all of you!"

A brief, startled silence followed his abrupt outburst.

Thony, with his usual superb sense of timing *(honed from years of practical jokes)*, let it build for a moment before continuing.

"You're always listening to *her* problems," he shouted at his stunned parents. "You *never* listen to *me*, or ask how *I* feel about stuff! And *you,*" he rounded on his sibling, "*you're* so busy mooning over *Jeremy* that you've lost what little brains you had!"

The pretty princess' eyes narrowed very *un*prettily and Thony hurried on, hoping he'd have the chance to apologize to her later. *Priscilla* wasn't the one he wanted to be upset at his tirade.

"You never even seem to remember that I *exist!*" he went on dramatically. "Some sister *you* are!"

As he said this, Thony very slowly and deliberately crossed his eyes at her. Because of their various positions at the table, Mama couldn't see, but Priscilla definitely could. She blinked in puzzlement and he could practically see the questions running through her mind. What was he up to? And why so suddenly?

"I hate *all* of you," Thony concluded, "I'm going to my room and don't *any* of you try to get me out, because I'm *never* coming out *again!*"

And he dashed out of the room before anyone could say a word.

But not before Queen Annabel had burst into tears and Priscilla had shot him a nasty look with a wink in it – she'd gotten the message all right!

The young prince paused as soon as he was out of sight and listened guiltily. Mama was weeping, and Papa was soothing her... but she actually sounded more upset that he'd 'reverted' to such immature behavior than anything else. He snuck away as Great-Uncle Sir Eddie began to pontificate on the Vagaries of Youth.

Keeping up the rather tedious façade, just in case anyone was watching, Thony ran all the rest of the way back to his rooms, slammed the door shut, and bolted and barred it. By the time he had caught his breath and gotten on with the next task, Priscilla had arrived though the servants' entrance to his bathroom. She had long ago discovered this was the safest way in to see him.

She discovered him contemplating a rather tall pile of... *stuff* on his bed.

"So, what's going on?" she asked, one fine, golden eyebrow arched curiously.

"Prissy!" Thony said with relief. He hastened over to give her a hug. "Listen, I'm really sorry for what I said before, but I was trying to make it sound real."

She waved his apology aside. "I thought it must be something like that. If for no other reason than I don't think you'd say something rude about *Jeremy* after all he's been helping you." She gave her little brother *two* raised eyebrows and he flushed.

"So, I say again," Priscilla continued. "What's going on?"

"I'm going to do what you did last year," Thony began.

"You're going on a husband-hunting quest?" the golden-haired Goddess of Love smirked. "Hoo, boy, but the gossips will have fun with *that.*"

He gave her a withering look. It had absolutely no effect, and he decided to practice his withering looks before using one again.

"No, of course not. Papa's been arranging to have me betrothed at my birthday party." He recapped the problem for her, finishing with, "The whole thing pretty much becomes a non-issue if it looks like I've disappeared. Roger become Papa's default Heir at that point as Joanna's husband, and *he'd* be supported by King Richie."

"Because to do otherwise would suggest that *Richie's* line isn't Blessed with the Divine Right of Kings either." Priscilla nodded. "And Roger's younger brother, Ryan, is just about to go rescue *his* princess-heiress, isn't he?"

Thony nodded. With *all three* of his sons – even the "ne'er-do-well" middle-born one – standing likely to become kings, he hoped that King Richie would be forced into a broader worldview... and that Papa would be able to forgive him if he was.

Priscilla stepped closer to the bed. "So. You're going to run off on your own Quest. And see if you can find a princess that you can actually love to bring back with you and make it clear that the Devinthal line isn't *cursed.* As *if.*" She rolled her eyes at that idea, then went on more seriously. "But you're planning on going all alone, Thony, and you're even younger than I was. And *I* had Joanna. And *Roger.* Who is a belted knight. *You've* had a month or so of half-lessons in sword and bow."

"Which were more to entertain Roger and Jeremy and stop me from complaining than any real use," Thony nodded. "I'm aware. I'd take someone with me if I dared. And I *swear* I'll be careful."

He could practically see the thought running through her mind that there weren't robbers anywhere near Aldyrwald, or even in the mountain region more generally until one got to the last couple valley-kingdoms at the edge. And that she was the Goddess of Love and could surely give him a Blessing to find his true love *long* before he reached those more dangerous places. Priscilla's face had always been an open book to her younger brother.

Luckily the reverse wasn't true, or he wasn't going to be able to pull this off.

She snorted slightly. "Despite what everyone else seems to think, you're the most careful person I know. I suppose you couldn't have survived all those practical jokes of yours if you weren't."

"I've never played a prank that was potentially fatal to *anyone.*" That was almost offensive.

"And you *know* that because you thought through everything in detail." Priscilla nodded. "You're careful, as I said." She looked at the pile on the bed. "*Too* careful, possibly. Are you running away or moving out?"

Thony winced. "It's all stuff I might need."

His older and more-experienced-at-traveling sister sighed. "You'll have two saddlebags. One is for food. The other one fits everything else. If it doesn't fit, it doesn't go. You can tie a roll of blankets for sleeping on the back of your saddle as well. But that is *it.*"

He sagged a bit in relief. "So, you'll help me."

"You helped *us*, didn't you?" She put an arm around his shoulders and squeezed. She was still a little taller than him since her last growth spurt that he hadn't caught up with.

"Thanks, Prissy."

"Don't thank me yet," she warned. "We've yet to pull this off. They'll search for you even harder than they did for us. You'll need a good head-start."

Thony nodded. "I have it all planned out. Mama and Papa will think I'm sulking in here–" His heart twinged a little at not letting her know that Papa was in on the Plan... but even Papa didn't know *exactly* what he was planning, and the confusion as they all had to figure out what everyone else knew would cause delays. She'd said herself that he needed a good head-start, right?

"– all I really need you to do is to get me some traveling food now and to empty the food-trays they'll leave at my door. They know I'd never sulk so much that I wouldn't *eat.*"

Priscilla nodded companionably. "Sounds reasonable. I'll extract you a traveling kit from the kitchens without anyone being the wiser. You... whittle that pile down while I'm gone." She frowned. "Do you even *have* saddlebags?"

Thony put on his best innocent look. "Yes."

She chuckled. "Well. I'm not going to ask how you managed to get them. I'll get your kit and be back in a jiffy." She looked at the gigantic mound again. "You need clothes – the sorts of things you'd practice riding in – and maybe a bar of soap, a tinderbox and striker, some money... that had better be silver and copper only and hide it in various places, don't carry it all on you in your purse."

Priscilla seemed ready to go on a bit more, but Thony nudged her towards the door. "Got it. And food and a waterbag and cooking supplies. And you're the one who can get me those."

She laughed and departed... and Thony pulled out the saddlebags that he'd hidden earlier under his bed. With his gout, Great-Uncle Sir Eddie would never need these again... and Thony had left coins to cover the cost of a new set if that should somehow change.

He began packing a reduced set that came out of the original pile in surprisingly little time and good order. While the rest of it was stuff he would *like* to take, he'd pulled it out mostly as camouflage... to make Prissy think he was utterly clueless. Thony had read enough stories of traveling – and he'd talked to everyone who'd traveled much that he could manage – so he thought he had a reasonable idea of what was wise to take.

Cloak and boots he would wear. Four shirts, two pairs of pants. Eight sets of stockings and underwear, since they packed small. A pair of shoes in case he ended up someplace where riding boots weren't appropriate. A pen with ink and notebook. The tinderbox and starter that Prissy had recommended, and the soap, though he stuck in two bars; he liked to be clean, no matter what Great-Uncle Sir Eddie thought. A comb. Several small knives. A compass and the very small folding spyglass that he'd talked Papa into getting for him from a trader when he was ten.

A sewing kit, with the extra set of leather-needles and awl and his darning egg. Thony had learned to sew and darn while he was a small boy playing underfoot in Mama's solarium. Although it might take a while, the point of this excursion was to find his princess, and that meant keeping himself in good order so he didn't look like a ragamuffin to be dismissed out of hand once he did. The sewing kit also contained a small pair of shears, as well as thread snips, and could be used to trim his hair if absolutely necessary.

And speaking of which... the shaving kit that Papa had given him for Midwinter and that he still hadn't had much need for had to go, since he likely would need it *eventually*. A small mirror to go with it, because he wasn't such an idiot as to consider putting a razor to his throat without a mirror to see what he was doing.

Shaving razor, scissors, knives... a sharpening kit was clearly called for. And that medicines pack he'd put together a few years ago – salves and ointments and bandages, some twists of tea for headaches and such. *(The castle doctor had been incredibly suspicious when Thony started inquiring about such things, but the young prince had managed to convince him that he was just being responsible. If he was going to create havoc, someone might get hurt and it was only the proper thing to have the wherewithal to help.)*

Money, all in coin, as Prissy had said. Printed money was only as good as the government that guaranteed it, and it seemed unlikely that any from Aldyrwald or the surrounding countries would do him any good where he planned to go. He *did* take some gold, despite her advice, though he hid most of the coins in the secret pockets he'd long ago added to his boots and belt, and planned to open some of the seams of his saddle to hide the rest at the first chance he got. Not that a robber mightn't just take his horse, saddle and all... and his boots for good measure; but there was only so much a person could do.

Amanita had managed somehow, traveling here. And she'd done it on her own, without the benefit of a trader's caravan or even a horse. Just the pack on her back and whatever she could carry. And she was a lot younger and smaller than him. Surely *Thony* could manage if *she* had.

The saddlebag was all but full, so Thony added a number of other small items that might come in handy and sealed it. Next were his blankets, rolled tightly into a waterproof tarp that he'd collected for a prank a few years ago.

One of those small items was his great-great-grandmother Arabella's engagement ring. Thony had liberated it from the castle Treasury on the same excursion earlier as when he was appropriating Great-Uncle Sir Eddie's saddlebags. It wasn't technically *stealing*, since – as the future King of Aldyrwald – it would all come to him in the end anyways... and, since the ostensible reason for his departure was to find a princess-bride, he'd need a ring to give the maiden when he gave up and picked out some girl.

And Great-Great-Grandmother Arabella's ring just seemed appropriate for some reason. She had been the Devinthals' first deviation from 'proper royalness' after all; Great-Great-Grandfather Anthony *(whom Thony was named for)* had rescued her from a pair of Evil Sorcerers before realizing that she was their *daughter* and *not* a princess they were holding captive. Which could have been nearly as bad a scene as what they now faced, once the truth came out, but no one had dared to suggest that Prince – and later King – Anthony didn't retain the Divine Right of Kings. Not with those two powerful *(and apparently not-so-evil)* sorcerers standing behind him as fathers-in-law.

Somehow the ring reassured Thony about his own prospects.

By that time Priscilla was back, arms laden. She helped him pack the second saddlebag, explaining what each item was, from jerky to the small cook pot and ladle. She'd even included a small jar of salt and another of sugar and several paper twists of spices that she said would be handy if he was trying to turn some of the leathery jerky into a more edible form by steeping it in boiling water. A second tiny pot was for tea. And a tri-pod of metal rods that could be stood up over a fire for one of the pots to rest on at a time.

The saddlebags were... rather heavier than he'd anticipated, but Prissy gave him a hand in sneaking them down to the stables.

It was dark out now, and the stablehands were out having their nightly bonfire. They were able to sneak into the barn and past the sleepy horses without raising a fuss, although Twinklestar *huffed* at Priscilla with some indignation. Silverfoot was as alert as ever, and had his ears up and an interested look in his eyes before Thony had even opened his stall door.

Saddle and bridle... saddlebags were new to Thony, but Priscilla knew how to attach them from her months on the road.

Months... she and Roger and Joanna had only been gone for less than four months, but Priscilla, in particular, had seemed to have gotten more than four months older. Thony had been putting it down to becoming a Goddess *(and maybe falling in love)*. But some of the things they'd said suggested that the Quest had lasted longer for them than it had for Thony. For *Aldyrwald.*

A relic of them having gone through the Fairy Wood? The usual stories about people being captured by fairies had them waking up in a much later *century* (either extremely aged or still youthful; it seemed to depend on the storyteller more than the tale) not just a few extra months or a year or something.

Hmmn. That likely meant Joanna was even closer to having the baby than Thony had thought. She'd only begun to look seriously pregnant recently, and she'd been gone so much lately that he hadn't really thought about how he'd be missing the birth of his first niece or nephew.

Oh, well, the kid would still be around when he got back.

Jeremy cantered in while they were working, handed the boy and Priscilla several items, ruffled Thony's hair, kissed Priscilla, and departed silently. The items turned out to be a bow and a quiver of arrows and a *sword.* Real steel with an edge and all, and the young prince wasn't sure it was at all a good idea to take along a weapon he wasn't sure he could properly use.

"Swords are expensive," Priscilla said very quietly as she noticed his dubious expression "If you can find someone to teach you a bit more, you should do that, but you'd never be able to afford to buy one. Same with the horse. Jeremy says you can handle the weapons well enough to do some good. And he's told Silverfoot that if anyone takes him away from you, he's to find you again at the first opportunity."

That... was very sweet of them. Thony hoped he could live up to all this.

Priscilla showed him how Roger had carried his sword and bow attached to the saddle, and then they made their way out of the barn, the horses around them continuing to sleep. It occurred to Thony that Prissy was probably responsible for that in Her Aspect as Goddess of Animals.

She was being more than helpful... which suggested *she* didn't see any other options either. Nor Jeremy, given that She had somehow communicated with him and he was going along with Thony's plan as well. Hopefully that meant She and Jeremy would make things all right with Joanna and Roger. There seemed to be an order of precedence among the new-made Gods but Thony wasn't sure if Priscilla had been acceding to Joanna's directions as a Goddess-Thing or as a Big Sister-Thing. Were Living Creatures – or Love – senior in importance to the Elements Themselves? Or the reverse?

Probably it was something he would never entirely understand...

"Take care of yourself, Thony," Priscilla said when they reached the edges of the circle of lamplight that surrounded the barn. "Come back soon. Oh! I miss you already!"

She gave him a warm hug and blinked hard several times.

Thony hugged her back. "Tell Mama and Papa and Joanna that I love them. And give Roger and Jeremy my thanks. And... I love you, too."

"And I love you... Good luck, little brother. May you find what you *truly* seek."

That... was really all there was to be said.

He mounted up and started Silverfoot away at a quick walk. Some of the harness was jingly at a trot or a canter, and it was really too dark for moving quickly anyhow. Thankfully, the waxing gibbous moon had risen and the road was clearly lit ahead.

Still... *someone* should know what he was really doing beyond the hints he'd scattered.

"I'll give your greetings to the Fairy Queen!" Thony called back, and stirred Silverfoot up to a faster pace before Prissy could do anything more than call out his name.

Or rather before She *Chose* to do anything more. Thony rather suspected that saving him from his own folly would count as something She didn't think She should use Goddess-

Powers for; a number of those deep discussions he'd sort of hovered on the edges of had included a great deal of discussion regarding the free will of mortal beings.

He did spare one backward glance for the castle where he had lived all his life.

But then he turned his eyes to the future and guided his horse in the opposite direction from all those morning excursions to the glen where he had met Roger and Jeremy.

This time he went towards the mysterious depths of the place that had absorbed his sisters and Roger a year ago – the Fairy Wood.

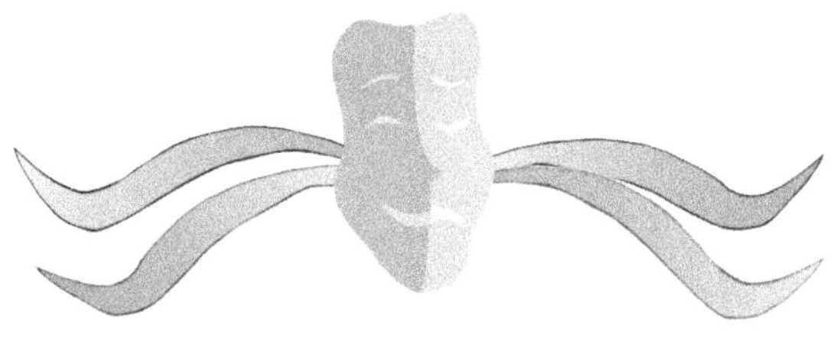

Chapter THIRTEEN

That *Idiot!*

AMANITA HAD JUST COME IN from the usual bonfire to check on Twinklestar before going to bed. She did it every night, not that he ever needed anything, but it was good manners. Her former mentor had given her good reason to remember her manners, especially in the matter of unicorns.

Twinklestar seemed somewhat more agitated than usual, and Amanita couldn't tell why at first.

When she heard the voice of Her Highness and Holiness, Princess and Goddess Priscilla the Fair, the reason for the unicorn's fussiness was obvious. Priscilla's visits always upset Twinklestar.

When the girl realized that Her Highness and Holiness was calling out Thony's name in a worried tone, the matter took on a different complexion entirely.

Uh-oh, the stablegirl thought to herself. She followed the sound of the Princess-Goddess' voice.

The older girl – the *Goddess* – stood just at the edge of the lamplight, staring worriedly out into the darkness where the road led off.

Amanita went up to her. "Goddess-Lady?" she asked humbly.

Where she came from, Goddesses were taken a great deal more seriously than they seemed to be here... though of course none of her own people had suddenly *become* a Goddess. There was some old hack about no one respecting you on your hearth-stone, no matter what amazing things you'd done in the greater world. Or *worlds*.

It was one of the reasons she wasn't really looking forwards to going home, no matter how much she missed her parents and her brother. And her cousins and aunts and even her *one* grandmother.

Not that she'd have a choice soon.

Priscilla blinked and looked down at her. The golden-haired young Goddess was reasonably tall and Amanita was short for her age in this land.

"Yes?" Priscilla offered, trying to focus on a potential supplicant, but unable to hide Her worry.

"My name is Amanita, Lady. I'm a friend of Thony's. What's he gotten himself into now?"

Priscilla regarded her steadily for a moment, and Amanita bore up under it. The princess was still new at this Goddess stuff, so it wasn't too hard, especially for someone like Amanita.

"He's running away," the Goddess said at last, "though *he's* calling it a Quest. If you know him that well, you'll know why." Priscilla gave her a sharper look and Amanita forced herself not to wince away. With this many Gods around, it had only been a matter of time anyways...

"Not just *know*, you'll *understand* why, won't you," Priscilla said thoughtfully. "And being who you are... and where you're from... You'll understand my concern when I tell you he's apparently decided to copy my sister and Roger and I, and go through the Fairy Wood."

Amanita did indeed. She slapped her forehead with her hand. "That *idiot!* He'll get himself killed! I have to go after him!" She frowned suddenly. "But he's on Silverfoot, isn't he. There's no way I can catch up to him by walking."

"You would follow him?" Priscilla was still giving her that intent look. Eyes that gentle and blue were never meant to be that *intent*. It was kind of spooky.

"That's what a *friend* does," Amanita said firmly firmly and before the Goddess of Love could impute any other motive to her. "He can't just go over to the other side alone. He could end up *anywhere!*" The girl frowned harder in thought. "I can't just *take* one of the horses," she muttered to herself. "Tad'll kill me."

Should she go get Wesley? The three of them had been a team the last several weeks and she'd miss the big lug. But Amanita knew where she was going – or where she'd be trying to go anyways. And Wes... would not be a good fit.

Neither would Thony, but apparently he was determined to try.

Among other things, once they were in the Wood, they'd have to stick *exactly* to the path she knew or they might get lost forever. The best she could hope for was to come out where she'd entered and that her mentor there would be able to send Thony back here not much the worse for wear. After making it through the Fairy Wood, *Thony* might listen to her about that. *Wes* wasn't likely to.

Possibly she could get Quellarie send *both* her and Thony back to Aldyrwald, but there were... *reasons* that Amanita might have to stay.

"Twinklestar will take you," the Princess-Goddess' voice broke into her thoughts. "He likes you already... you *are* the one who takes care of him, aren't you? I didn't think there was more than one girl who worked in the stables."

"I am," Amanita confirmed a little dazedly. "I mean – you mean I *can*? I can take him? Except – no. No, I can't. I... may not be coming back here and Twinkie's *your* unicorn."

Priscilla winced. "No, he's not. Not the way you mean, anyways. Not that he didn't offer, but we hadn't got it sorted out before all... *this* happened. We're not bonded, unicorn to maiden. But it's up to him. Take him if he'll go. Perhaps he won't have the same problems with you that he does with Me."

Amanita knew exactly what *that* meant.

"He won't!" she exclaimed dramatically. "I'd die first! I'm never..." her voice faltered. She had about as much choice about that as Thony did. And for pretty much the same reasons.

Priscilla sighed. "Never is... a very long time. Even unicorns usually understand that. With Twinklestar... it's mostly that we never really had a chance." She pulled a somewhat pained smile out of somewhere. "I can see that right *now* you never want to go all 'icky' and fall in love with someone – or get married."

"No offense intended, Goddess-Lady," Amanita said a little faintly.

"None taken." The Goddess of Love shook her head. "You and Thony. You really are a pair. In that neither of you wants to find your true love," she explained as the girl began to feel alarmed. "Even if that's the pretense for *his* quest."

Amanita felt like she was wasting time. She knew where Thony was headed, she had transportation now – she didn't really think Twinkie would refuse her – and she needed to get going. She took a step backwards towards the stable.

"I'll make sure he doesn't permanently injure himself, Lady," she said, taking another step. "And that he comes back here as soon as possible." She paused thoughtfully. "Temporary injuries he likely couldn't avoid if he tried."

Priscilla snorted in a very un-God-like and unprincessly way. "Truer words have never been spoken. Thank you. I'd go myself if I weren't Bound here now... and I'll give you the same Blessing that I gave him: may you find what you *truly* seek," She said before Amanita had time to grow *really* alarmed.

The girl relaxed slightly. That seemed general enough not to be more of a burden than she was willing to bear.

With a polite bow, she turned and dashed to the barn to explain the situation to Twinklestar.

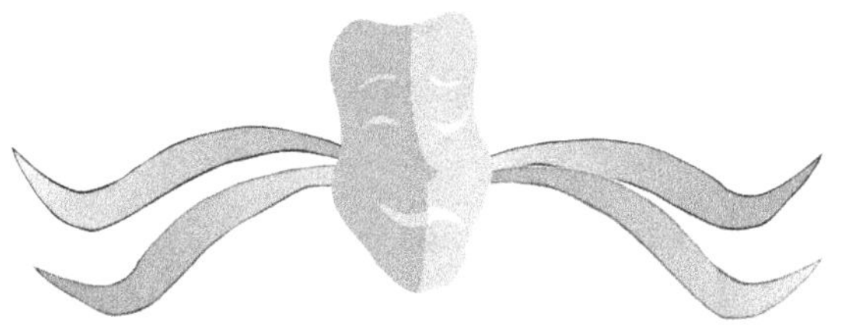

Chapter FOURTEEN

Carnivorous Plant People!?!

THONY SLOWED SILVERFOOT DOWN ONCE Prissy was out of sight. If she'd meant to stop him, she could have, and she hadn't. So that suggested that she'd decided to support him with his Crazy Plan. And that meant there was no reason to risk his horse getting injured in the dark.

The road *should* be smooth enough to not make it much of a risk, but Thony wasn't as familiar with the highways on this side of the castle, having been relegated to the more innocuous ones that led to the glade where he'd been meeting his brothers-in-law. This one continued along the way to Schwannsberg – Roger's homeland – and past the Devinthals' castle in the other direction, to Eidersparg.

And it just *happened* to run alongside the Fairy Wood for a few miles a league or so out of sight of the castle.

Thony might not have traveled this road himself, but he'd studied it from the top of the castle wall, and he knew the map of Aldyrwald as if it was the back of his own hand. Since he hadn't been permitted to investigate his own Realm-to-be, it had been all he could do...

He'd resented being held back like that for so long that it was hard to let go of the feeling, even though *now* it was blatantly obvious that King Bill and Queen Annabel had been thinking about their options for a very long time indeed. And how to manage those options for the well-being of both Aldyrwald and their children. If Thony – at a year too early – was a hot item on the royal marriage market *now*, he'd likely have been an attractive *kidnapping* target earlier on.

Kidnapping... to raise him as the foster-son of another king and then returned as the 'long-lost Heir', and happily – or *un*happily, but unequivocally – married to a foster-sister, an appropriate princess from the other country.

Or... *assassination*, leaving Joanna as the Princess-Heiress and available to the other king's youngest son to wed.

What a mess.

But at least he knew a good spot to make a camp at the edge of the *normal* part of the forest.

Only an idiot would try to enter the Fairy Wood at night, after all.

If his Plan held and Prissy was able to distract their parents for even *half* of tomorrow, it would be fine. And since Papa knew Thony was planning *something*, presumably he'd delay the search himself.

Thony had left letters for Papa and Mama. He'd marked them for the post and put them in the bin where all the outgoing mail was collected if it wasn't being sent by special messenger. Hopefully someone would think to check there before the mail was taken away from the castle and sent on... but even if it wasn't, he'd addressed them to Roger at his parents' castle in Schwannsberg. Either Roger would stop in and be given the missives, or else Queen Janet would have them sent back to Aldyrwald.

And on the off-chance that someone in Schwannsberg – like that nosy Princess Tessa *(she'd been 'rescued' but the sedding wasn't till next month, so she was back home)* – decided to open the packets, there were envelopes inside that were properly addressed to his parents. And sealed with his own signet ring, which should give even *Tess* pause in trying to peek inside.

He didn't want Mama and Papa to worry more than absolutely necessary, after all.

Thony found the spot he'd marked mentally – there was a small side-trail that led behind some rocks and bushes to a little glen with a stream. It was an established camp for riders, with a fire-ring of rocks and an area clearly marked off for horses so that there wasn't much chance of finding horse-apples in or near one's bedding-down place.

He sort of wanted to try making a fire, but there was no real need, it being a very mild night for late Spring. And a campfire might give him away if things were less controlled back home than he'd planned for.

Thony tethered Silverfoot in the designated area and removed saddle and saddlebags, saddleblanket and bedroll. Setting up a space for himself to sleep didn't take very much longer.

The young prince stretched himself out on his back and stared up at the stars winking at him through the partial canopy of Spring leaves and still-bare branches. He'd carefully put the tarp underneath him and two layers of blankets to try to keep the ground from stealing his warmth. His cloak and another layer of blankets were over him and he hadn't bothered to remove any more clothing than his belt and boots, so he should be warm enough.

It was real.

He'd done it.

Or... almost done it.

Until he was actually *through* the Fairy Wood on some other world, it was still arguable whether he'd *done* anything of particular note.

And then there would be the whole problem of finding his princess. And convincing her that he really *was* a prince. And to come back to his own world with him. And then convincing the surrounding royalty that *she* was a princess and that therefore the Devinthals really *did* still have the Divine Right of Kings...

Mostly problems for another day. Thony wasn't all that concerned about the first few issues. Despite not having asked Priscilla for any sort of formal Blessing, the young prince was reasonably sure She had given it to him anyways.

Likely he couldn't *avoid* finding his true love if he tried.

And if it was true love, she'd come back with him. Because that was what true loves *did*, wasn't it?

He sighed deeply into the darkness, listening to Silverfoot exploring the available pasturage by taste.

Girls – besides his sisters – were an annoyance *(though, honestly? the boys he knew really had nothing to recommend them either. Except maybe* Wes. *And Amanita. But they were clearly not typical)* and it was absolutely ridiculous that he should be forced to measures this extreme just to find some acceptable maiden who wasn't *old* and likely to want to *off* him. Hopefully this 'true love' thing worked the way it was supposed to or he'd be stuck indeed.

He'd closed his eyes in a determined attempt to get some sleep, when noises from the direction of the road suggested he was about to receive company.

Thony tensed in unhappy anticipation and sat up to pull his boots on. It sounded like a single person and horse, so perhaps it was just a messenger coming in.

Or worse, one going *out*, if Queen Annabel had discovered he was gone and insisted on sending someone to Schwannsberg immediately. It made a certain amount of sense that Thony would flee there, given that he knew Roger's family somewhat well. Perhaps it might even be assumed that he'd heard about the plan to marry him off and had run away to plead for Tess' *(rather encumbered)* hand. Or even Sophia's.

Even if it wasn't either of those, however, this could get a little hairy. Doubtless every messenger – and knight and farmer and even traders who passed through Aldyrwald – knew that the crown prince wasn't allowed out. Let alone at night and alone. Even if they didn't try to force him back home *(or decide on a more nefarious plan, such as holding him hostage for money)* they'd be likely to mention Thony's location to his parents. And likely they'd realize something was off because he *didn't* have a banked campfire... which meant they might try to pretend they hadn't noticed anything strange and would sneak off with word of his whereabouts once he was asleep...

The only option was to act nonchalant and try to get on the road – and into the Fairy Wood where he couldn't be traced – before the other person woke up in the morning.

Putting his boots on was probably utterly useless, though he'd prefer to have a shot at running if the newcomer proved to have dark designs. No one outside of Aldyrwald should know he had run away yet and they had no tradition of noble bandits – the cessation of hostilities across the mountain region a few centuries ago had done away with most cases of excessive taxation – which was the whole excuse for the existence of noble robbers – but there was always the possibility of an ambitious young upstart trying to make a name for himself. There were too many tales of those noble bandit-types winning an heiress' hand and inheriting lands and wealth, after all.

A few tense moments later, Thony relaxed and settled back down. He didn't take off his boots, though. That irritated voice could only belong to Amanita, but *she* had no reason to be out here either. Had she heard him depart and was coming to talk him into going back?

Thony was startled to see the small girl's dark, shadowy shape come stumping into the little clearing followed by the glowingly white hide of Twinklestar. There wasn't a great deal of moonlight making it in past the trees that were just getting really leafed out, but the unicorn didn't seem to need to *reflect* light from the heavens.

"Would it have *killed* you to make a fire, Thony?" Amanita grumped. "It's as dark as the underside of a horse's tail out here."

As if to emphasize her point, she stumbled slightly. The girl caught herself on Twinklestar's mane, resulting in an unhappy *whinny* from the unicorn and a toss of his head.

Oh, wait. She hadn't caught at his *mane*. She'd grabbed the *reins*. And if that was a bridle with a bit – and Thony wasn't aware of any hackamores that were available in the royal stables; the bitless bridles were a style he'd only read about – then that probably had *hurt*. Twinklestar might never have had a bit in his mouth before and was surely allowing such a thing only as a favor...

"Sorry, Twinkie," Amanita apologized in a tone of horror.

Thony was up in the instant and was easing the bit out of Twinklestar's abused mouth. Much like the stableboys, he hadn't particularly wanted to make a Big Deal of how well he got along with Priscilla's unicorn-friend, but there was no one but Amanita here to see and comment. Not that Thony had any interest in doing anything that would discourage Twinklestar's interest; it was just that he didn't see a need to be snickered at by a pack of boys, most of whom were as innocent as he himself but inclined to harass him over it.

And then if the *squires* found out... Papa didn't hold with his squires bothering the servingmaids, and the noblemaidens were all holding out for marriage proposals. But somehow the older squires all ended up with those smug expressions as they started spending more time with the hired knights, and trying to emulate the older men. Thony *wasn't* so innocent as not to be able to guess that they'd made it past first kisses with *some*one... and likely it was *some*one who wouldn't get the Wrong Idea and whose father wouldn't have the leverage to successfully sue for a proper marriage or indemnity. And if those older boys felt they were justified in such behavior with their meager – or non-existent – inheritances, they'd think Thony a fool for not using his much vaster resources to elicit even more such, um, *attentions*.

Getting away from all of that nonsense was surely another benefit of this running away business. Even if the arguable *point* of his departure was to find himself a princess.

Better not to think about that too hard or it would take all the joy out the expedition.

"Are you alright?" he asked the unicorn.

Twinklestar's response was another toss of his head, but he added a somewhat mollified whicker and rubbed his head against Thony. His attitude towards the penitent Amanita was less forgiving, but he suffered them to work together to remove the saddle and blanket and saddlebags that had been strapped onto his back. Ignoring the girl entirely, Twinklestar then turned with horsey disdain to head over to Silverfoot and enjoy a bit of a graze, perhaps while snoozing. Unicorns might be magickal creatures, but they were built like horses and needed to eat just about as constantly.

"He's not going to let me forget that," Amanita said, sounding like she was wincing. "Not for awhile anyways. Even though he agreed that it would be easier for him to cast the spell to hide his horn and look like a pony while we're traveling if he had a bridle and reins."

Thony folded his arms. It was hard to see much of her – the moonlight was all but gone, and really all the light was from Twinklestar's hide.

"I'm assuming your departure from the castle is entirely coincidental. Are you going back home?"

The girl made a snort that was half a snicker and set about arranging her things to setup a place to sleep. "Yeah. Probably. At least if you're doing what your sister said you're doing. You need a guide if you're going through the Fairy Wood, and given the dearth of other options, it looks like I'm it."

He was not going to let his jaw fall open in shock. He'd guessed that she'd traveled in to Aldyrwald from the Fairy Wood. He had. *Really*.

Okay, no, he hadn't. Not at all.

"You come from somewhere on the other side of the Fairy Wood?" Thony demanded.

Amanita paused and turned her head in his direction. "Um. Yeah. Right. The *'other side'*."

She went back to fussing with what were probably blankets. It was too dark for him to tell.

Thony rolled his eyes. "Another *world*. I've listened to my sisters and Roger and the centaurs. I know the Fairy Wood takes you to places that aren't accessible by just riding around the outside edges of it."

There was a longer pause.

"Hunh. You're smarter than I thought."

"Thanks," Thony said dryly. "Where exactly are you from again?"

"A place," she hedged. "Um. In the mountains. Don't worry about it. We aren't going *there*, though I *will* get us back to my home world. You have to be super-careful in the Fairy Wood," she said seriously. "If you go left around certain trees instead of right, say, you end up in totally different places. Like, different *worlds*. Or even differnt places on the *same* world. And it's not always possible to re-trace your route. And some of those places are supposed to be super-dangerous. Like all lava and burning stuff or air that's poisonous or carnivorous plant-people. Stuff like that."

"Carnivorous plant people?" the young prince exclaimed. He wasn't sure if it was with dismay or disbelief or... discouragement. Dis- something anyways.

He'd guessed there would be danger; like robbers or outlaws or scam artists. But this was a whole other level than he'd planned for.

"I haven't actually seen any of that," Amanita admitted. She seemed to be settling down to sleep. "Quellarie told me how to get the help I needed to get *here* and after she told me about the other places, I decided not to experiment a great deal."

'Not a great deal' didn't sound like 'not at all'. But it also sounded like she'd had enough of a scare to let her fairly decent amount of commonsense surface.

Thony sighed and resigned himself to having her along on his... well, he *could* call it a Quest, couldn't he? And... actually, the idea of having a friend with him – and a guide – was sort of appealing.

Of course, now he'd have to take *care* of her and make sure she got wherever she was going safely. Even if it weren't the Proper Princely Thing to help a Damsel in Distress, Wesley would just about kill him if Thony let anything happen to Amanita.

Which probably meant he needed to find a way to get her back to Aldyrwald, eventually, as well...

He sat back down and pulled his boots back off.

"So... Her Goddessness didn't actually tell me a lot of details about *why* you decided to run off all of a sudden," Amanita said as he closed his eyes. "Can I assume this has to do with that plan of your parents to get you married off on your birthday?"

"Betrothed, not married," Thony muttered. "They can't make me marry anyone until I'm *six*teen."

"Whatever." Amanita dismissed the distinction. "Getting half-hitched isn't much better than fully hitched. You planning on coming back here later on?"

"Of course!" Thony was a little shocked that she might think otherwise... though he agreed with her assessment else.

"It's gonna be the same mess when you come back," she pointed out reasonably.

He sighed. "Not if I can find a princess somewhere else. *Anyone* would be better than one of the jerks who lives around here – or one of their Princess-Aunts – and who has an incentive to get rid of me and Papa both so her country can absorb Aldyrwald." He paused. "I assume there are princesses where you come from."

There was a rather... *long* silence.

"Yes," Amanita said at last. "There are princesses. And princes. And lots and lots and lots of other people. *Lots* of *non-princess*-type people," she added with a certain emphasis.

"Well, *I* need to find a princess," Thony replied. "If I bring back even a worthy miller's daughter it'll be a mess."

"Hunh." Amanita sounded... less skeptical and more sympathetic than he would have expected, given her rather strong views on egalitarianism. "Well, good luck. I'll help you get through the Fairy Wood at least. I don't know that I can really help with the rest."

She sounded like she was hedging again. Did she know a princess in her homeland that she didn't want to introduce Thony to? And was that because she was friends with *him*... or friends with *her*?

Well, it hardly mattered. At least he'd give it a good try. If he didn't find anyone on Amanita's world, he could always come home and see if he could sneak off to the edges of the mountain-region to find an appropriate girl. Maybe Uncle Louis and his former-mermaid princess knew a king who would be more open-minded.

Honestly, going off to their country *now* would have been a better plan if he weren't mortally sure that Mama would never let him get that far. Or Joanna and Roger. Or... King Howard of Liepbaum or any of their other neighbors who stood to gain by leaving Thony and Aldyrwald stuck in this impossible situation.

"All right," Thony said. He thought again about *carnivorous plant people* and poisonous air and places that were nothing but burning. "And, um, thanks."

"No problem," came the answer. "Get some sleep. We're gonna need it."

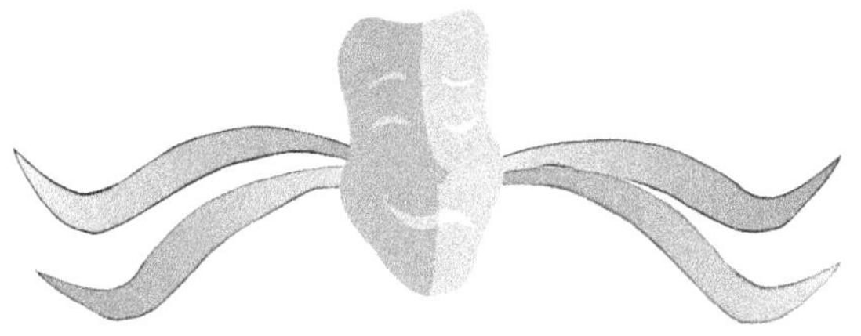

EPILOGUE

Free at *Last?*

THEY ENTERED THE FAIRY WOOD early the next morning as dawn was still painting peaceful shades of pale pink and yellow across a perfect blue sky. As Amanita had commented, grouchily, without even a banked fire to prepare a decent breakfast there wasn't much point in sitting around to eat hardtack and cheese. They could do that just as well a-saddle.

Thony didn't really appreciate the superior attitude she was taking about everything, but he couldn't argue that she *was* the more experienced traveler. No matter how much it irked him.

Hopefully she'd get a little less bossy after she wasn't hungry and this might actually end up being fun.

He paused Silverfoot just before they went all the way under the tree canopy, and looked back at Aldyrwald.

The castle wasn't visible from here. Just acres and acres of neatly tended fields and pastures dotted with fluffy looking sheep. A good-sized stream – Starling Brook – wended its way across the peaceful landscape.

It was calm and lovely.

And unutterably boring.

Thony fought down a last twinge of guilt over the worry his parents were going to feel. He was doing the responsible thing. The only *possible* thing to save Aldyrwald from their greedy neighbors.

"Hey, *dude*. You coming or not? The Fairy Wood might wait all day, but *I* won't."

The young prince sighed and turned away from home to follow his ferociou– erm, *feisty* little friend into the *deepest*, *darkest*, and most *dangerous* place he'd ever gone.

...

(Not that that was a high bar.)

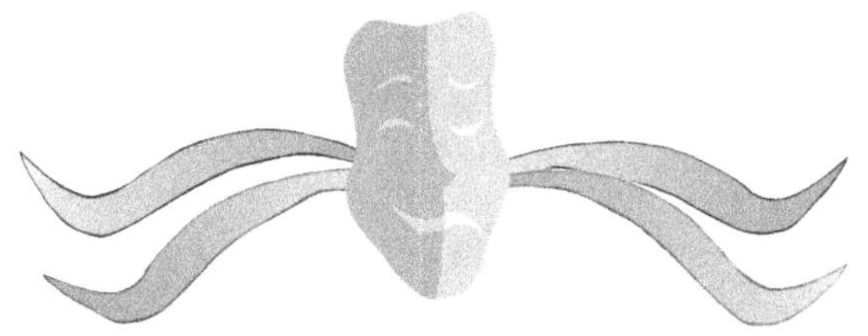

Index of Characters and Places

- Aldyrwald. The country where Thony is Crown Prince. Three linked valleys, centrally located in the mountain region.
- Amanita. A foreign girl who works in the castle kitchens.
- Annabel (Queen Annabel of Aldyrwald). Wife of King Bill; mother of Joanna, Priscilla, and Thony. Youngest of seven sisters and three brothers.
- Anthony (former King of Aldyrwald, now deceased). Husband of Queen Arabella, great-great-grandfather of Thony.
- Arabella (formerly Queen of Aldyrwald, now deceased). Wife of King Anthony, great-great-grandmother of Thony.
- Bill (King Bill / King William Devinthal of Aldyrwald). Husband of Queen Annabel. Father of Joanna, Priscilla, and Thony. Oldest of seven brothers.
- Caspar. Stallion of the centaur herd that inhabits Aldyrwald. Mate of Mariah, sire of Jeremy.
- Dave (Grandpa Dave). Queen Annabel's father; husband of Grandma Marybeth. Former king – he abdicated in favor of his oldest son. Thony's grandfather.

- David. Son of the Chief Cook in the Aldyrwald royal kitchens. Something of a genius at making soups. (Amanita calls him 'Mr. Make-the-Stew').
- Eddie (Great-Uncle Sir Eddie / Prince Edward of Aldyrwald). A middle-born brother of King Bill's father, Grandpa Tom. Thony's riding master.
- Eidersparg. One-valley kingdom in the mountain region, located adjacent to Aldyrwald.
- Eswith (Master Eswith). Protocol master of the Aldyrwald royal family.
- Howard (King Howard of Liepbaum). Father of middle-born Princess Stella.
- Janet (Queen Janet of Schwannsberg). Wife of King Richie; mother of Prince Raymond, Prince Sir Roger, and Prince Ryan, Princess Laura, Princess Sophia, and Princess Tessa.
- Jeremy. Centaur male. Husband of Priscilla. Son of Caspar and Mariah.
- Joanna (Princess Joanna Devinthal the Wise and Wonderful). Eldest-born princess of Aldyrwald. Daughter of King Bill and Queen Annabel; sister of Priscilla and Thony. Wife of Prince Sir Roger. Goddess of the Earth.
- Joe (King Joe). Queen Annabel's oldest brother.
- Laura (Princess Laura of Schwannsberg). Oldest daughter of King Richie and Queen Janet; younger sister of Crown Prince Raymond; older sister of Prince Sir Roger, Prince Ryan, Princess Sophia, and Princess Tessa.
- Liepbaum. Two-valley kingdom. Nearby, but not immediately adjacent to Aldyrwald.

- Lizzy (Grandma Lizzy / formerly Queen Lizette of Aldyrwald). Mother of King Bill widow of King Tom. Thony's grandmother.
- Louis (Uncle Louis / Prince Louis of Aldyrwald). King Bill's youngest brother (last of seven). Prince-consort of a coastal country.
- Luke (Master Luke). Artistic chandler who lives in Aldyrwald.
- Mariah. Lead mare of the centaur herd that inhabits Aldyrwald. Mate of Caspar, dam of Jeremy.
- Marian (Princess Marian of Eidersparg). Fifty-something middle-born sister of the king of the one-valley kingdom of Eidersparg.
- Marybeth (Grandma Marybeth). Former queen. Mother of Queen Annabel; wife of Grandpa Dave. Thonys grandmother.
- Milt (Prince Sir Milt of Aldyrwald). One of King Bill's middle-born brothers.
- Paul. Journeyman pastry chef in the Aldyrwald royal kitchens. (Amanita calls him 'Mr. Grabby-Hands')
- Priscilla (Princess Priscilla Devinthal the Bright-Eyed and Bushy-Tailed, aka Prissy). Second-born princess of Aldyrwald. Daughter of King Bill and Queen Annabel; sister of Joanna and Thony. Wife of Jeremy. Goddess of Animals (including humans) and of Love/Fertility.
- Quellarie. Someone who advised Amanita.
- Raymond (Prince Raymond of Schwannsberg). Crown Prince. Son of King Richie and Queen Janet. Older brother of Prince Sir Roger, Prince Ryan, Princess Laura, Princess Sophia, and Princess Tessa.

- Richie (King Richie of Schwannsberg). Husband of Queen Janet. Father of Prince Raymond, Prince Sir Roger, Prince Ryan, Princess Laura, Princess Sophia, and Princess Tessa.
- Ronnie (Prince Sir Ronnie of Aldyrwald). One of King Bill's middle-born brothers.
- Roger (Prince of Schwannsberg and Knight). Second-born son of King Richie and Queen Janet; younger brother of Prince Raymond and Princess Laura; older brother of Prince Ryan, Princess Sophia, and Princess Tessa. Husband of Joanna. God of Air.
- Rosie. Thony's tired old mare.
- Ryan (Prince Ryan of Schwannsberg). Youngest son (of three) of King Richie and Queen Janet; younger brother of Crown Prince Raymond, Prince Sir Roger, Princess Laura, Princess Sophia; elder brother of Princess Tessa.
- Schwannsberg. Two valley kingdom immediately adjacent to Aldyrwald.
- Silverfoot. Thony's more energetic horse.
- Sophia (Princess Sophia of Schwannsberg). Middle-born daughter of King Richie and Queen Janet; Younger sister of Crown Prince Raymond, Prince Sir Roger, Princess Laura; older sister of Prince Ryan and Princess Tessa.
- Stella (Princess Stella of Leipbaum). Middle-born daughter of King Howard.
- Tessa (Princess Tessa of Schwannsberg). Youngest child (third daughter) of King Richie and Queen Janet; younger sister of Crown Prince Raymond,

Prince Sir Roger, Princess Laura, Princess Sophia, and Prince Ryan.

- Tad/Thaddeus. Stablemaster to Aldyrwald Castle.
- Thony (Prince Anthony Devinthal the Affable and the Affirmative). Crown Prince of Aldyrwald. Younger brother of Princess Joanna and Princess Priscilla.
- Tom (formerly King Tom of Aldyrwald, now deceased). King Bill's father; Grandma Lizzy's husband. Thony's grandfather.
- Twinklestar. Princess Priscilla's unicorn-friend.
- Wesley (Wes). Stableboy in the Aldyrwald royal stables.

Also by Kerridwen Mangala McNamara

YOUNG ADULT Fiction:

- ***Thony and the Much-Anticipated Adventure***
  Book One of The Prankster Prince
- ***A Not-So-Sacrificial Maiden*** .
  Book One of the Knightess of the Realm

More YA coming soon...

- ***Thony in the Deep, Dark, Dangerous Fairy Wood***
  Book Two of the Prankster Prince

ADULT Fiction:

- ***The Rebel Duchess*** .
  Book One of the Chronicles of Ilseador

More Adult coming soon...

- ***A Not-So-Simple Mission*** .
  Book Two of the Knightess of the Realm
- ***The King's Champion*** .
  Book Two of the Chronicles of Ilseador

Non-fiction:

- ***The Homeschooling Parent*** .
  Self-care and Feeding of the Person Who Makes It All Happen

More non-fiction coming soon...

- ***One Plus Three Equals Zebra-Pants*** .
  Bringing Math to the Math-averse (parents and kids both!)

Author's Note

This inaugural book of the Prankster Prince series is near and dear to my heart. Most of it was sketched out when I was about sixteen – probably the funniest parts. At that time I had a very supportive pair of friends to share stories (mine and theirs both) with… and I can't entirely take credit for developing some of the characters that will be showing up. Certainly some of them were improved (or made less like me, which is all to the good for developing more interesting characters) by the many discussions we had, sitting in each other's rooms as teenagers.

The biggest helpers this time around, however, were my kids. They LOVE this story and keep encouraging me to write more. This book is a bit shorter than some of the others… *they* wanted me to add a bit before moving on to Book Two, but Thony and Amanita's adventures in the Fairy Wood seem like they deserve a book of their own.

(They are also responsible for most of the improvements in the story - pointing out such Issues as that if humans are animals, then Amanita *did* meet a 'talking animal', and that those mops were probably dripping on someone's head.)

While this book practically flew off my fingertips (except for the formatting, that's a bear), the process of finishing it was complicated with a uniquely kid/YA problem: chickenpox. While only two out of the five kids who were home caught it (it began over Spring Break and the oldest decided to stay away instead of visiting for a few days), nonetheless it changed all our patterns of behavior.

My first thought was a greedy excitement: quarantining ourselves should have meant that I had more writing and less driving-around time. I've actually been "missing" the pandemic as we have filled our lives back up with playgroups and Lego teams and model government teams and university lectures and fencing and archery and so on. (Not actually missing it, of course. Not only would that be callous, we've had Covid three times ourselves, despite care and vaccinations and long-covid continues to impact several of us. And we were lucky to not have other concerns. But I miss how much less structured our time was during the lockdowns.)

It didn't quite pan out that way because of a different family health-crisis: my beloved father-in-law, Shawn McNamara began a relatively sudden, rapid descent. Writing doesn't happen when one is grieving or anticipating grief. And he was one of the best people I have ever been given the gift of knowing. We rushed to Tucson for his Celebration of Life just as we finished our chickenpox quarantine.

I would be remiss not say a few words about how awesome my father-in-law was. Shawn was the kind of man everyone wishes was their dad – fun and firm and eternally optimistic and supportive and open-minded. He raised five kids of his own – and numerous daughters-in-law, grandchildren, foster-children, and friends-of-children who needed a safe and welcoming place for a night or many nights. Five years ago, he biked from Santa Fe, New Mexico to Cleveland, Ohio to attend his fiftieth high school reunion – after having heart surgery. Shawn always had a baby in one arm if there was one around and small children (and larger ones) would cluster around his kind and understanding presence. He could fix a car or add on to his home and was always available to help move – or just plain help – anyone and everyone. And even when we saw Shawn back at Christmas time, when he was between surgeries and looking rather iffy as he used a walker to get around without a functioning knee-joint, he had not the slightest doubt that he would be back on his bike in a few months. He and my sweet and amazing mother-in-law celebrated their fiftieth anniversary last Fall – just after my husband and I celebrated our twenty-fifth. Family – in all its best possible incarnations – was what Shawn was all about.

I had to dedicate this book to my kids – it was written FOR them in many ways, after all. But it has to be co-dedicated to my father-in-law. Because. Just because.

RisingDragonBooks

About the Author

Kerridwen Mangala McNamara is an Indian-American with a Master's degree in Bacterial Genetics who lives in Flyover Country (the far northern end of the US South) with her husband, The Professor, four of her six children, and three goats. The goats eat, The Professor plays chess, and the children largely unschool while Mangala writes. (The remaining children are in college – you can blame the oldest for the excessive amounts of math showing up in Mangala's fantasy novels, the second one for better attention to staging of scenes, the third for all the economics, and the fourth for great attention to history – and all of them for a focus on political science!) Mangala is a former professional bellydance instructor, currently coaches FIRST Lego League and model government teams, runs homeschool parent support groups, and used to enjoy knitting, crotchet and embroidering Temari balls but now is much more boring as she rarely does anything but write, argue economic theory with her 17 and 14 year olds, and wonder loudly if her 11 and 9 year olds do anything other than watch Minecraft videos. She owes her love of books and reading to her mother, who was a professional folklorist and could recite – from memory – stories from every nation in the United Nations.

www.ingramcontent.com/pod-product-compliance
Lightning Source LLC
Chambersburg PA
CBHW070358200726
48294CB00003B/974
9781960160096